To Rebecca —
Israel Gerber

Isadore Waber

U2 Can Grow Up To Be . . .

U2 Can Grow Up To Be . . .

Isadore Waber

Copyright © 2008 by Isadore Waber.

Library of Congress Control Number: 2007907966
ISBN: Hardcover   978-1-4257-9031-8
                   Softcover   978-1-4257-9021-9

All rights reserved. No part of this book may be reproduced or transmitted in any form or by any means, electronic or mechanical, including photocopying, recording, or by any information storage and retrieval system, without permission in writing from the copyright owner.

This is a work of fiction. Names, characters, places and incidents either are the product of the author's imagination or are used fictitiously, and any resemblance to any actual persons, living or dead, events, or locales is entirely coincidental.

This book was printed in the United States of America.

Graphic Design—Sam Leonard

To order additional copies of this book, contact:
Xlibris Corporation
1-888-795-4274
www.Xlibris.com
Orders@Xlibris.com

Helen, Debbie, Abigail and Sam

Introduction

It was Tuesday, election day, the day that would determine which candidate would emerge victoriously, with a mandate to govern for the next four years. Traditionally, voters vote for candidates whose philosophical views and opinions are in accord with theirs. On the right are fiscal conservatives, candidates who stress individual initiative with minimal interference from government. On the left are liberals with a philosophy that government has an obligation to help individuals who need the help of government to provide the basic necessities of life. In between are the issue voters with strong concerns on such issues as abortion and gun control. This election was different. The weather was favorable. Skies were sunny across much of the nation. On this Election Day voting was unusually heavy. Polls reported long lines throughout the day. The heavy turnout was not a result of the favorable weather. The heavy turnout was triggered by an expose in a special edition, five days before the election, by Tell Publications, profusely illustrated with explosive photographs.

Tony Brentwood, the Republican candidate, led throughout the campaign and was expected to win handily. That was the situation that existed up to five days before the election. An expose changed the dynamics. The election could now go either way. It was a highly charged, emotional revelation that skewered all conventional voting patterns. There were voters who would have voted for Tony Brentwood, but switched because of the expose. No way would they want this man in the white house. Pollsters were unable to assemble information that would provide a basis for a reliable prediction of the outcome. Exit polls were too vague, too confusing to be of value. Tony Brentwood and the Republican Party worked furiously to control the damage, with some success. The timing of the expose was too close to the election to give them the time they needed to calm the turbulent waters. Tony Brentwood's lead had narrowed, but to what extent was impossible to know. The Republicans were hopeful that they could pull it out.

The Democrats kept a low profile. Although they benefited by this changed situation, they prudently distanced themselves from the highly emotional atmosphere. Professionals were all in agreement that dawn would be breaking before the winner could be identified. This would be an election that would question the moral and legal right of a publisher to invade the privacy of a person's home in order to obtain photographs that would be damaging to that person. Tell Magazine was primarily sold in super markets, and it targeted prominent people with sensational reporting of events in their private lives. In this issue the Republican front-runner, Tony Brentwoood, was the target.

The Democratic standard bearer, Alfred A. Mitchell, was photographed with his wife, Martha, casting their ballots. Alfred spent the rest of the day making appearances at various functions. It was early in the evening and he finally returned home. It had been a very tiring day. The entire campaign had been an exhausting, grueling experience. This was the end of his ordeal, Regardless of the outcome the physical demands of the campaign were over. Alfred had two choices. He could go to Democratic Headquarters and monitor returns as they came in, or he could hit the sack and get a good night's sleep. It had been an exhausting campaign and he was dog-tired. He elected to hit the sack.

As Alfred A. Mitchell took off his pants, he thought of the unusual set of circumstances that led to his being the Democratic choice for president. He didn't want to be nominated. What the hell did he know about being the president, or about politics? He wouldn't be disappointed if Tony Brentwood was declared the winner. With this new revelation he could find himself on top. He campaigned hard. He did everything he was told to do. If he loses, they will know he did his best. Tony Brentwood was a tough man to beat. The hell with it. Whichever way it goes, it's out of his hands. Let the voters decide, and that's what they've been doing.

Alfred thought back to the set of circumstances that led to his being nominated. As interim president of Grigsby Crowbar, he was identified as being the guy who made all those strategic moves that rescued the company from disaster to a brilliant recovery. Admittedly, he made all the bad decisions that almost wrecked the company. It was Dave who jumped in and turned the whole thing around. He told them, but they wouldn't listen. They brushed it off. He was modest and self effacing. What could he do? The convention was deadlocked and they wanted a compromise candidate without political baggage. When the chairman of the party tells you that it's your patriotic duty to accept the nomination, how the hell can you refuse? He sure could use a good night's sleep. During the day he was handed two scripts; victory and concession. Whichever way it goes, the hell with it.

Alfred thought about the series of events that got him to this stage in his life. It was as a caddy that he first met Elmer Grigsby, the president of Grigsby Crowbar. Elmer was a duffer, a most untalented golfer. When he hooked a ball into deep rough, Alfred dropped a ball onto the fairway and told Elmer that the ball had ricocheted off some trees and landed on the fairway. He shouldn't have done that. Caddies don't do that. On future outings he realized that Elmer didn't give a damn about scores. He just enjoyed the smell of freshly cut grass, the singing of birds, and a day free from office pressures. His real passion was restoring antique cars. Alfred had a good relationship with Elmer, he was like a father, and it was inevitable that he would become an employee of Grigsby Crowbar. Over the years there were advancement to better positions. He was manager of the mail room, manager of the parking lot, and manager of maintenance. He also was manager of stockholder relations.

His big regret was the mistakes he made that were so disastrous for the company, and caused so much pain and anguish for Elmer. All of that could have been avoided if he had only listened to Elmer. The office of executive vice president had to be given to someone with years of experience and a very strong educational background. That's what Elmer said. He should have listened. So he didn't listen and insisted he could handle it. Elmer, very reluctantly, gave in and appointed him with the stipulation that it was temporary, only until such time as they recruited a qualified person. What a disaster. He was sure Elmer would suggest that he find employment elsewhere. Instead, Elmer made him his special assistant. In Elmer's eyes he was still that kid who caddied for him. So he promotes Dave to the executive V.P. And Dave does one hell of a job. He really, single handedly, made Grigsby a great company.

So, the Democratic standard bearer picked up his pants and draped them over a chair. He sat on the edge if the bed to remove his socks. And there was Martha. Her two addictions were bargain shopping for clothes, and the Tuesday night bridge games. He didn't know how the hell she would adapt to living in the White House. No way would she get involved in causes like sponsoring the annual Girl Scout cookie sale, or the Red Cross drive for blood donors. Tony will probably pull it out, so why worry. The guy they really wanted was Dave. They just wouldn't listen. With Elmer's retirement Dave will be president of Grigsby. That meeting he had with Dave; very embarrassing, very demeaning. Dave really let him have it. "You're the interim president only until I have a successor. I don't want you to make any decisions, Take long vacations. Play golf every day, but I don't want you to make any decisions I'll have to deal with when I take over." He really used a sledgehammer. He could have been more diplomatic. That's the way he wanted it. No big deal.

Alfred A. Mitchell, suitably pajamahd, slipped under the covers and was soon fast asleep. It had been a grueling campaign, an exhausting day, and he was mentally and physically dog-tired. At this point, the outcome of the election was of very little concern. What will be will be. Tony Brentwood, the Republican standard bearer, had been coasting to victory. With only five days to election, he was involved with post election planning. That was prior to the Friday when Tell Publications went public with its special issue. This was a devastating development, and the Republican Party was in disarray. At a hastily called meeting, it was decided that Tony would ignore the expose and talk about issues that were of concern to the electorate. The hard hitters in the Party would blast Tell Publications and discredit them for their sleezy policies. Tony Bentwood spent Election Day with various supporters, and planned to spend the night at Republican headquarters to monitor returns. At dawn, Doug Carson, a bleary eyed broadcaster, announced "we have a winner.

So this was how it was on Election Day. And this is how it was with Alfred A. Mitchell on the months preceding the election.

Chapter One

GRIGSBY CROWBAR CORPORATION

Inter-office memo

To: Elmer Dexter Grigsby 2nd
President / Chairman of the Board

From: Alfred A. Mitchell
Executive Vice President

Subject: "We can cut our phone bills" campaign.

Before I get into this telephone project, I just have to congratulate you on the way you guided us through the difficult job of restructuring our company. I'm sure your grandfather would have been mighty proud. The decision to close down the Dayton plant wasn't easy. You accomplished this and still found time to devote to your very interesting hobby of restoring antique cars.

Thanks to your leadership, we are well positioned to do business in the twenty-first century with our core products, the finest line of crowbars anywhere on this planet. Our motto "Grow with Grigsby crowbars" has never been more meaningful. Now, about the "We can cut our phone bills" program. There are some expenses that are time related. What I mean is that if you call our lawyer and ask him if it's OK to quote Abraham Lincoln in an advertising piece, you get a long winded legal opinion and a hefty charge for the time he spent on the phone. We just don't realize that time is money. It's just too easy.

We have about a thousand telephones throughout our organization. So we buy a thousand three minute egg timers and place one beside each telephone. With each call made, the timer is flipped and the call is timed. It's no big deal. Our people will be more than happy to co-operate. It will work because it's simple and uncomplicated. You don't even have to plug anything into a wall socket.

> Your comments, please.

GRIGSBY CROWBAR CORPORATION

Inter-office memo

To:		Alfred A. Mitchell
		Executive Vice President

From:	Elmer Dexter Grigsby, 2nd
		President / Chairman of the board

Subject: "We can cut our telephone bills in half" campaign

I don't know about this one. I don't think our telephone bills are out of line, and the last thing I would want to do is to inhibit our employees. The telephone is a useful tool in doing business, and that's what counts. It doesn't bother me if some employee calls his bookie to place a bet on the third race. Traditionally, Grigsby is a relaxed place to work. It's been that way since grandfather founded the company, and I want it to continue. That having been said, if you want to put a timer beside every telephone, I won't object, provided you make it very clear that they are free to use the phone as they have in the past. Nothing has changed. Don't put one beside my phone! I am not sold on this one. I still remember the "Cheese and crackers, eat at your desk, sweepstakes," fiasco. Forgive me for bringing it up.

Anyway, thanks for your kind words about the restructuring. It took place the same time as the restoration of a rare Stutz Bearcat was nearing completion. This magnificent automobile is now the flagship of my collection. Not for long. I have just come into possession of a very fine Pierce-Arrow. This fine auto was up on blocks for over sixty years. I came into this automobile through very unusual circumstances. The original owner was Thelma Breckenridge, of the railroad family. She and grandfather; well, that's another story.

I really can't see any purpose for this telephone thing. It's OK, but only if our people are made to understand the importance of the telephone, and that they are encouraged to use the phone as they have in the past.

Law Offices

Costello, Nearing, Bream and Foster
666 Cassius Drive
New York, N.Y.

Mr. Robert T. Benton
Purchasing Agent,
Grigsby Crowbar Corporation
1 Whitemarsh Circle
New York, N.Y.

Dear Robert:

I have given careful consideration to the proposed purchase of one thousand egg timers. In my opinion there would be no involvement with the Environmental Protection Agency, or the Occupational, Safety, And Health Administration since an independent contractor did the manufacturing, off shore. Also, there would be no conflict with union contracts since the outsourcing provisions would not apply. The egg timers are not to be incorporated into any of Grigsby products.

The union was advised of the pending purchase, and after two intensive meetings where every aspect of Grigsby's contractual responsibilities were reviewed, the union agreed with our position that this was a one time purchase, atypical of Grigsby procurement requirements. You can issue a purchase order for these units. When you receive the timers, please send us ten units so that we can be assured of safe usage.

Very truly yours,
Gerald R. Bream

GRIGSBY CROWBAR CORPORATION

Inter-office memo

To: Alfred A. Mitchell
        Executive Vice President

From: Robert T. Benton
        Director of Purchasing

Subject: "We can cut our telephone bills in half" program

You will be pleased to know that I issued a purchase order to the Far East Import Export Company for one thousand egg timers imported from Touliaza. They have these timers in stock so delivery will be prompt.

According to company policy, for a purchase in this category, I will be submitting samples to our attorneys, Costello, Nearing, Bream and Foster, for their evaluation. Also, our engineering department will be checking the units to make sure they are as ordered. I don't anticipate any problems, and as soon as I get clearance, the timers will be released for distribution.

Law Offices

COSTELLO, NEARING, BREAM, AND FOSTER
666 Cassius Drive
New York, N.Y.

Mr. Robert T. Benton
Grigsby Crowbar Corporation
1 Whitemarsh Circle
New York, N.Y.

Dear Robert:

I have received the egg timers I requested, and sent them to Singleton Laboratories for analysis. Upon inspection they found that the decorative painting was applied with a lead based paint. Although there is little danger that this could affect the user, it is their opinion that the paint should be removed as a safety precaution.

Singleton Laboratories recommended that the paint be stripped from the wooden surface. This work would be done in a facility with an approved ventilation system. Since strong solvents are used, the fumes would have to be dissipated through a system meeting federal standards. Singleton recommended a company where this work could be done. They were contacted and advised of the problem. After examining the samples, they sent me the enclosed estimate. As you can see, the cost is sizable. Driving up the cost is the need to mask the glass portion of the timers. If this were not done the solvents would etch the glass portion, making it impossible to see the sand moving from one compartment to the other. After the paint is removed, the timers would be coated with a heavy varnish to seal in any particles of paint embedded in the wood surface. Delivery would be five to six weeks.

After delivery, you may safely make distribution of the egg timers.

Very truly yours,
Gerald R. Bream

GRIGSBY CROWBAR COMPANY

Inter-office memo

To: Robert T. Benton
        Director of purchasing

From: Ralph Esposito
        Director of Engineering

Subject: "We can cut our telephone bills in half" campaign

I'm sorry that we couldn't get to this program sooner. We were so involved with the development of our new line of collapsible crowbars, we neglected other important programs. The new line of collapsible crowbars is now in the capable hands of our sales department, and I understand that they are getting an enthusiastic response.

All of us in engineering are supportive of the program to substantially reduce our outlay for telephone service. Making the telephone company rich is not the mission of the Grigsby Crowbar Corporation. We have completed our examination of the egg timers. Here are our findings.

The egg timers were received for our evaluation. We found that it is incorrect to assume that the time that it takes for the sand to be transferred from one chamber to the other to be three minutes. In our examination we found that the elapsed time ranged from two minutes, twenty-seven seconds to four minutes and eight seconds. No egg timers, in our sampling, registered three minutes. All of the testing was done within acceptable, controlled environmental standards.

Since the units are sealed, we did not want to disassemble the units without proper authorization. As a result of careful observation, and whatever other measurements we were able to make, it is our opinion that the grains of sand, and the diameter of the opening which permits sand to pass from one envelope to the other, and the sizes of the envelopes, are a constant. In our opinion, the variations can be attributed to the quantity of sand at the point of assembly. Apparently no standards were maintained as guidelines for the assembly people at the point of origination.

Because of our findings, these units cannot be properly referred to as three-minute egg timers. As a further test, we boiled a dozen eggs (jumbo size). As the sand ran out, an egg was removed and carefully cracked open. At the conclusion, we found, the condition ranged from watery, not solidified, to solid whites, but not hard-boiled. The results have been documented, and are a part of this report. Our engineering department is at your service. We can pursue a more intensive investigation, and possibly take corrective measures if authorized.

GRIGSBY CROWBAR COMPANY

Inter-office memo

To: Alfred A. Mitchell
        Executive Vice President

From: Robert T. Benton
        Director of Purchasing

Subject: "We can cut our telephone bills in half" program

I am enclosing reports from our attorneys and from Ralph in Engineering. Our lawyers are not approving the use of the timers without the removal of the lead, in accordance with the provisions specified in the enclosed estimate. Ralph's findings pinpointed the diversity in the amount of sand flowing from one envelope to the other. I realize that we already have spent a considerable sum just in the involvement of our attorneys. To go ahead with this project, to have the work done on the timers, would greatly add to the cost of the program.

I called Gerald Bream to see if there would be some other way of handling this. He said the work had to be done. He further said that if we decided to abandon this project, I should contact him to make sure that the timers would be disposed of in accordance with Environmental Protection Agency regulations. He did suggest that we consider the cost/reward figures to see if this program is worth pursuing.

This is the situation with egg timers, Please advise.

GRIGSBY CROWBAR CORPORATION

Inter-office memo

To: Robert T. Benton
        Director of purchasing

From: Alfred A. Mitchell
        Executive Vice President

Subject: "We can cut our telephone bills in half" program

We didn't buy these goddam timers so our employees can boil some lousy, rotten eggs. And we don't have any stupid employees who would lick the paint and get lead poisoning. No way are we going to throw money away by having the paint removed. They are to be used to monitor telephone calls, and for that purpose, they are three minute egg timers, period. All the lawyers are interested in is making money and protecting their asses. Our president is upset because of the delays, and escalating costs.

Let's have no more of it.

Please release these timers for distribution to our people. We can't afford any more delays, and we certainly don't want any more of this meaningless nit-picking. Do it and do it now.

Chapter Two

+GRIGSBY CROWBAR COMPANY

Inter-office Memo

To: Alfred A. Mitchell
Executive Vice President

From: David Lambert
Director of Sales

Subject: "We can cut our telephone bills in half" campaign

We received our allotment of timers, and I have to congratulate you on this brilliantly conceived campaign to cut our telephone costs. With one hundred percent cooperation from our employees, I'm sure the savings will be dramatic. Our telephone bills can be cut in half.

Because of our present involvement in introducing our new line of collapsible crowbars, we, regrettfully, will have to delay our participation in this worthy campaign. I have given this a lot of thought and came to the conclusion that, for now, we just couldn't introduce another element to our already involved commitments.

We have been very busy meeting with our sales people in regional meetings worldwide. The successful introduction of our new line of collapsible crowbars is dependent on our ability to educate our sales people and customers in the principles that make the collapsible crowbar a unique tool for leverage lifting.

The telephone has always been a very important sales tool for us, and I assure you, we always use it judiciously. You are to be complimented for this unique and creative program. When we get the collapsible crowbar properly launched, we'll get on it immediately. You'll have our complete cooperation.

GRIGSBY CROWBAR CORPORATION

Inter-office Memo

To: Elmer Dexter Grigsby
         President, Chairman of the Board

From: Alfred A. Mitchell
         Executive Vice President

Subject: "We can cut our telephone bills in half" campaign

I'm enclosing a copy of Dave's memo to me in which he states, flat out, his refusal to participate in the timer program. Dave is not a team player. No company can be successful without the co-operation of all employees. We announced the timer program as a company wide effort to achieve a specific goal. It is not the prerogative of any of our management people to choose what company directive he will or will not support.

I just thought this should be brought to your attention.

GRIGSBY CROWBAR CORPORATION

Inter-office memo

To: Alfred A. Mitchell
        Executive Vice President

From: Elmer Dexter Grigsby
        President / Board Chairman

Subject: "We can cut our telephone bills in half" campaign

I can understand your frustration in not getting Dave's cooperation at this time. Although I can sympathize with you, it may be better not to judge him too harshly. The introduction of our new line of collapsible crowbars is about the most important promotion we've been involved with since this company was founded. It has special significance since getting acceptance for our collapsible crowbar will help tremendously in conditioning the market-place to look with favor when we introduce our newly developed collapsible camping shovel, to be introduced in the spring. Dave has been working very hard, doing everything in his power to assure the successful introduction of our new line.

I have had my eye on Dave for some time. He is a brilliant young man, very well organized, and he is an inspirational leader, able to generate enthusiastic response from his salesmen. Orders are coming in at a fast rate. No question. He's doing better than even I had hoped. Obviously he's capable of far more responsibility than he now has.

Recognizing his potential, I wanted to make sure that he stays with Grigsby. I called him in and let him know that, in my opinion, he was being under-utilized. I thought that his responsibilities could be broadened, and that there was a good future for him at Grigsby. In the next ten days I will announce his new title as Vice President for Marketing and Sales. He understands that this promotion will lead to positions of added responsibility in the future.

About this telephone thing, I'm sure it will work out OK. It's no big deal, not worth losing sleep over. Just relax, and let it run its course.

GRIGSBY CROWBAR CORPORATION

Inter-office memo

To: Elmer Dexter Grigsby, 2nd
        President / Board Chairman

From: Alfred A. Mitchell
        Executive Vice President

Subject: Organization of Sales Department

Dave has done a great job in introducing our new line of collapsible crowbars. For this he is to be commended. No question about that. What has concerned me is the "at what cost." He has been conducting meetings in ballrooms of the most expensive hotels, all over the world. Supporting these meetings are lavish feasts and top-flight entertainment. I crunched some numbers to get a handle on what it is costing Grigsby. The results were startling. To maintain a captive sales force, we are committed to maintaining a fleet of automobiles with the collateral expense of maintenance. We pay our salesmen generous salaries, bonuses, health insurance, meals, and stays at Four Star hotels. It goes on and on.

There is another approach to this problem that may be well worth exploring. What I'm referring to is the possibility of using the services of a manufacturer's sales agency. They charge a flat fee, usually about five per-cent of sales. All operational expenses, travel, cars, health insurance, entertainment etc. are their responsibility. We will no longer need to maintain a captive sales force. Since they represent other manufacturers, they are able to compensate their people adequately.

I think it's well worth considering.

GRIGSBY CROWBAR CORPORATION

Inter-office memo

To: Alfred A. Mitchell
Executive Vice President

From: Elmer Dexter Grigsby

Subject: Manufacturer's Agents.

I don't think so. Back in 1982, when my father was running the company, it was suggested to him that we pull the plug on our sales department and go the agency route. Savings could be substantial. It was a disaster. Sales plummeted. Dad, very quickly, recognized the problems and did an about face. It took a while to reassemble the sales people, but he did. We have a carefully honed sales staff; they're doing a great job, and I'm very proud of them. Sales agents may be good for the next guy, but not for us.

It may seem that Dave is spending money injudiciously, but that is not the case. All of the expenses spent by the sales department were carefully budgeted, and Dave is within his budget. He's doing a terrific job, and he has my enthusiastic support.

Employing the services of sales agents, for us, is not a good idea.

GRIGSBY CROWBAR CORPORATION

Inter-office memo

To: Alfred A. Mitchell
        Executive Vice President

From: David Lambert
        Director of sales

Subject: "We can cut our telephone bills in half" campaign

Good news! I think you will be happy to know that we have made distribution of the three-minute egg timers to our people, and they enthusiastically endorsed this program. Already we are seeing good utilization of the egg timers, and I'm sure the sales department will make a good showing toward the success of this well conceived program.

All of the people here at sales join me in congratulating you and our president for giving us the opportunity to contribute to the success of the "We can cut our telephone bills in half" campaign.

THE GRIGSBY CROWBAR COMPANY

Inter-office memo

To: Alfred A. Mitchell
        Executive Vice President

From: Jerry Silverman
        Director, Public Relations

Subject: Danny Gilbert Show

First, I'm sure you're familiar with the Danny Gilbert show. It comes on at 10 P.M., and from that point on it practically owns television. It's the most watched program in that time period.

I had a meeting with Danny's producer with a view to getting exposure for Grigsby on their show. What seemed to work would be to have four beefy men, standing on a platform, and being raised by our collapsible crowbar. We envisioned the four men to be the front four of the San Francisco Forty-niners; in uniform. Operating the collapsible crowbar would be the new movie star, Patty Lupescu. She recently starred in the new, sensational movie "It's OK to Laugh." She was superb and is now the most talked about star in Hollywood. We would use the Model AK-43 whose rating is sufficient to assure a safe lift of the load.

The producer checked their agents and we were given the costs (enclosed) for their appearance on the show. As you can see, the cost is quite sizeable. However, when you factor in the number of viewers the cost is within reasonable limits, per viewer. The exposure time for this segment is estimated to be seven minutes.

Millions of viewers will see this segment, and will think of Grigsby in a positive way when they think of crowbars. Normally, I wouldn't consider this type of exposure for our company. It has to be very tightly controlled, and I've taken every precaution to make sure nothing goes wrong. If anything did go amiss, Danny's like a loose cannon and can and does tear a visitor to shreds. Without very tight control it would be risky to participate in this show. Danny does respect restrictions that are part of the contract.

GRIGSBY CROWBAR CORPORATION

Inter-office memo

To: Jerry Silverman
        Director, Public Relations

From: Alfred A. Mitchell, Executive Vice President

Subject: Danny Gilbert show

I watch the Danny Gilbert show, from time to time, so I'm familiar with it. I guess I'm by nature a night owl, and just find a million things to do before I finally hit the sack.

Anyway, what you suggest could be of value to Grigsby. I must say I was floored when I saw what these people get for a brief appearance I guess that's show business. What occurred to me was that we could accomplish the same results without the use of these people. What the front four San Francisco forty-niners have to offer is their weight. From my observation, there are fat ladies among our employees who would weigh in about the same as the forty-niners. We pick out four fat ladies, use them, and the next day they're back at work. We save all those big bucks.

As far as this Patty gal goes, I think it would be fitting if our president used the crowbar. It would be great. He is charismatic and would be an asset to the program. When we have all our ducks in order, I will ask him.

Another point. I think using the AK 43 to lift the platform is not really needed. I'm suggesting the SS 21, a sleeker looking crowbar that could accomplish the lift. I would suggest we have the crowbar chrome plated for a flashy look.

Other than these minor changes, I agree, this would be good for Grigsby.

GRIGSBY CROWBAR CORPORATIOM

Inter-office memo

To: Alfred A. Mitchell
Executive Vice President

From: Ralph Esposito
Director of Engineering

Subject: Danny Gilbert Show

I had a conference with Jerry Silverman. He was particularly concerned about the change of crowbars to be used in a forthcoming demonstration, under consideration. He told me that the Model AK43 was changed to the SS 21. He described the load to be lifted; the front four of the San Francisco forty-niners. The use of the SS 21 crowbar completely wipes out the margin of safety, factored into the load specifications for that model. The use of the SS 21, taking into consideration the load to be lifted, could very well be disastrous. I would urge you to go into this project with the use of the AK 43. You just can't afford to take risks in this situation. It could be devastating, especially in front of a nation-wide audience.

Again, play it safe, go back to the AK 43. You don't want to be playing Russian roulette with our company's reputation.

GRIGSBY CROWBAR CORPORATION

Inter-office Memo

To: Alfred A. Mitchell
Executive Vice President

From: Jerry Silverman
Director of Publicity

Subject: The Danny Gilbert show

I am going to call the producer and tell him that we decided that our involvement in the Danny Gilbert show would not be appropriate for us. Before I do so, I wanted to let you know why I came to the conclusion that, participating in the show, would be disastrous for Grigsby.

I strongly object to the use of the women, our employee. We don't discriminate as far as weight or any other physical problem. Management respects our employees. Knowing Danny Gilbert's mind-set, he could very well have the women costumed in tu-tus, and in his monolog would refer to them as fat broads. That is why I stipulated very tight controls over our participation in the show. Without tight control our women would suffer humiliation, and the good name of Grigsby would be seriously damaged. We don't do that to our employees. They have always been respected in our company. This is outrageous.

In, addition, I received word from Ralph Esposito strongly objecting to the use of the SS 21. He said that the safety factor would be completely eliminated. To use it under these conditions would be courting disaster. What I had proposed was educational. With these changes, it's slapstick comedy. It's the sleeziest kind of entertainment. To involve our president and our employees in this tawdry business is unthinkable. To denigrate the good name of our company is not going to happen on my watch.

This is why I decided that the best interests of our company would be served by walking away from participation in this show. We don't need it, and we certainly don't want to do anything that would damage our company's good name.

GRIGSBY CROWBAR CORPORATION

Inter-office memo

To: Jerry Silverman
Director of Publicity

From: Alfred A. Mitchell
Executive Vice President

Subject: The Danny Gilbert Show

Jerry, I know exactly how you feel, and I appreciate your comments. I have watched the Danny Gilbert show for a long time. I know how he operates. He is entertaining, funny, but never vicious. As far as the women are concerned, they are well aware of the costumes that could be prepared for them, and they will probably be referred to in an uncomplimentary way. They understand that they are free to withdraw if this is offensive to them.

As for the SS 21 is concerned, it's a sleek, well-proportioned crowbar, and I feel that it is built well enough to do the lift. I am confident that the show will be entertaining and will go off as planned. I see no reason to be worried.

This offers us good exposure, and we're getting it at low cost. All I can say is "On with the show."

GRIGSBY CROWBAR CORPORATION

Inter-office memo

To: Alfred A. Mitchell
      Executive Vice President

To: Jerry Silverman
      Ex Director of Publicity

Subject: Resignation from the Grigsby Crowbar Corporation

Please accept this letter of resignation from the Grigsby Crowbar Corporation, effective immediately. I want it expressly understood that in no way did I make any contribution to the planning and format of the forthcoming Danny Gilbert program, as outlined in your memo to me. All of it is the work of the Executive Vice President, Alfred A. Mitchell.

I have cleaned out my desk and am leaving the premises for good. Again, whatever takes place on the Danny Gilbert Show, I had absolutely nothing to do with it. You, alone, will be responsible for whatever happens on the show.

Goodbye.
Jerry Silverman

GRIGSBY CROWBAR CORPORATION

Inter-office memo

To: Elmer Dexter Grigsby
        President / Chairman of the Board

To: Alfred A. Mitchell
        Executive Vice President

Subject: The Danny Gilbert Show

We are scheduled to demonstrate our new collapsible crowbar on the Danny Gilbert show, the nineteenth of this month. Jerry Silverman first arranged the program. In his proposal, he suggested hiring some football players, to stand on a platform, and some famous movie star to handle the crowbar. I was floored when I saw what it would cost us. These people were asking for a fifty-five gallon drum filled to the brim with twenty-dollar bills. I thought that the proposal was good, but the high cost unacceptable.

To get around this problem, it occurred to me that we could select four very obese women to stand on the platform and have our esteemed president do the honors with the crowbar.

I'm sorry that I won't be around to witness this program. As you know, I'll be on vacation. Martha and I will be on a cruise visiting the Greek Islands.

GRIGSBY CROWBAR CORPORATION

Inter-office memo

To: Alfred A. Mitchell
   Executive Vice President

To: Elmer Dexter Grigsby
   President / Chairman of the Board

Subject: The Danny Gilbert Show

No, Alfred, this is not for us. I'm not much of a television watcher, so you'll excuse me if I admit that I haven't the foggiest idea who Danny Gilbert is. What I do know is that I don't like the changes that were made. We respect our employees, and the last thing I would do is exploit them because of some physical abnormality. I don't care what the abnormality, whether it's excessive weight or a wart on the nose. When they work for Grigsby, management and fellow employees alike respect each other. Jerry Silverman can set you straight on this. Talk to him, and, by all means, cancel our participation in it. We don't want that kind of publicity. Publicity is Jerry's job. He can explain to you the boundaries of good taste, what is acceptable and what isn't.

On another matter, I need assistance in some matters that I'm involved with, so I'm promoting you to join me. Your new title will be "Special Assistant to the President." There's a room a couple doors from mine. It's presently being used for storage. I'm having it cleaned out, and it will be furnished by the time you get back. I'm promoting David Lambert to the office of "Executive Vice President." We had a long chat; and I'm really excited about this appointment. He's chafing at the bit, eager to get started. On your return, he will be working out of your old office.

Congratulations to both of you, and enjoy your vacation.

GRIGSBY CROWBAR CORPORATION

Inter-office memo

To: Elmer Dexter Grigsby
President / Chairman of the Board

To: Alfred A. Mitchell
Executive Vice President

Subject: The Danny Gilbert Show

I called the producer of the Danny Gilbert Show to cancel, as you suggested. He transferred me to their legal department. They had previously sent over papers to be signed. I was told that by signing the papers, I was being guaranteed that the slot on the nineteenth was being reserved for our firm, and no one else would have use of that time slot. At that time, I was certain, in my mind, that we would be demonstrating our new crowbar. I had no thought about canceling. I was told that this was a typical form, used in the entertainment industry. It protects them for expenses, such as costumes, and last minute maneuvering to get substitutes to fill the time slot. I realize now that I should have had our lawyers look at the papers before signing them.

Their lawyer told me that I could cancel, but they'd have to be compensated, and the penalties are very steep. I can understand how you feel about this exhibition. Under these circumstances, it would probably be best to go through with it. It's only seven minutes and we're out of there.

GRIGSBY CROWBAR CORPORATION

Inter-office memo

To: Alfred A. Mitchell
        Executive Vice President

From: Elmer Dexter Grigsby, 2nd
        President / Chairman of the Board

Subject: The Danny Gilbert Show

Fax the papers you signed to our attorneys, and let's see if they can get us out of this mess. If they can't, then we'll have to go through with it or pay the penalty. I don't know what our involvement is. Our lawyers will advise me. Whatever the cost, we should pay it and cancel. If we have to do this thing, I want Ralph Esposito to check every phase of the demonstration; the platform, the collapsible crowbar, and the costumes for the ladies. I don't want them put into any costume that would give them a bizarre appearance.

I'll be there on the nineteenth, if I have to, holding my nose. This should never have happened.

Chapter Three

It is the nineteenth. Alfred is happily on vacation, cruising the Greek Islands. Elmer is unhappily enduring a seven-minute show that seemed to him to be seven hours. Everything was wrong. He was shocked to see the ladies in tutus. A smiling Danny Gilbert was reeling off "fat broad" jokes in staccato fashion. He had the audience roaring with laughter. Elmer didn't think they were funny.

Not only did the sight of the ladies in tutus devastate Elmer. He was really upset when he noticed the size of the crowbar. He had expected the AK-43. He had asked Alfred to have Ralph Esposito check all aspects of the lift; the platform, the crowbar, and every other detail. He couldn't understand why Ralph would find the SS-21 acceptable. What Elmer didn't know was that Alfred did call Ralph, in accordance with Elmer's instructions, Ralph's secretary told Alfred that Mr. Esposito was off that day. It seems that Ralph's daughter was on the hockey team, and this was the big game, the game that would decide the championship. Alfred never did get around to call back. He was otherwise occupied. He could have asked the secretary to have Mr. Esposito call him when he returned. He didn't think of it.

Nothing that was going on was acceptable. Certainly the crowbar was the wrong size for the lift, the grotesque appearance of the ladies in tu-tus, and the inane yacking by Danny Gilbert. This was as much as Elmer could take. He had to pull the plug. He couldn't use the crowbar. It would be putting the ladies in an unsafe situation. If the crowbar collapsed, they would be thrown, and possibly suffer serious injuries. The crowbar was not safe to use. He would explain this to them and he was sure they would understand. No one would want to do something that could cause others serious inpjury.

Elmer looked around for someone to explain why it would be dangerous to use the crowbar. Then all hell broke loose. Everything happened so fast. He suddenly realized that the focus was on him. They were at that point in the show where Elmer would be demonstrating the crowbar. A man appeared in the wings, waving his arms frantically and jumping up and down. Then Danny Gilbert came running over with some other people, and they were all shouting and demanding that he use the crowbar. He tried to explain to Danny the serious problem with the crowbar, but Danny was a raving maniac, not about to discuss anything. The audience was screaming its head off. Elmer felt intimidated. With a firm grip on Elmer's collar, Danny unceremoniously propelled Elmer to the platform. He soon found the questionable crowbar in his hand. The audience was screaming. They thought that Elmer's reluctance to use the crowbar was a part of the show. Things happened fast. The atmosphere was chaotic, the noise deafening. Elmer had no recollection of actually using the crowbar. He was sure he hadn't. He was sure he couldn't. Were his hands on the crowbar? Were the hands on the crowbar Danny's? With the crowd, Danny and his assistants, it was impossible to identify the hands on the crowbar.

Later, Danny Gilbert told associates that this was one of the best shows they ever had.

Law Offices

COSTELLO, NEARING, BREAM, AND FOSTER
666 Cassius Drive
New York, N.Y.

Mr. Elmer Dexter Grigsby, 2nd
Grigsby Crowbar Corporation
1 Whitemarsh Circle
New York, N.Y.

Dear Elmer:

I watched the Danny Gilbert show, last night, and was sickened by Danny's audacious exploitation of the unfortunate failure of the crowbar. He fired up the audience and made them feel they were watching slapstick comedy. When the crowbar collapsed, and the women went flying in all directions, I feared that the women would suffer serious injury. I checked the hospital, and the women are being held overnight for observation. I understand that they are badly shaken, but, miraculously, there were no injuries. There is a possibility that some law firm will see this as fertile ground for a lawsuit.

When the market opened, this morning, the exchange quickly suspended trading on Grigsby. The sell orders probably created a problem. It would be expected that the widespread publicity of last night's event has shaken the confidence of some investors. There is nothing we can do about that. It's just unfortunate that, by mistake, the wrong model was shipped.

The one bright spot is the actions being taken by your new Executive Vice President; Dave Lambert. I had a long talk with him, and he is really on top of this situation. He was up all night making plans to contact customers, and rally all the employees to put this incident behind them, and look forward to a great future with the finest crowbars available anywhere. He sounded like the coach at a rally before the big game. I was really impressed.

I know you are taking a beating with an unforgiving press. The media is having a ball with what is really a tragic event. The "fat broad" jokes are not funny, and the Media ought to be ashamed of itself. I think you need to be shielded from all this unpleasantness, and I will be in contact with a public relations firm. More about this, later.

Very truly yours,
Gerald R. Bream

News Report

Grigsby Judge Sends Picketers Packing

Elmer Dexter Grigsby 2nd, beleaguered president of Grigsby Crowbar Corporation, was relieved of some of the intense picketing that he had been subjected to by women's groups, most notably by the newly formed "Fat Broads of America." Also protesting was the union. Under section 3-B, it should have been consulted with regard to the use of the four women in overtime, and also for a change of work classification. Judge Willoughby, of the third circuit court, issued a ruling restricting the number of pickets blocking the entrance to the building. The pickets were also restricted to a distance no closer than twenty-five feet. Bullhorns were prohibited because of complaints from others in the area with no connection to the Grigsby Corporation.

Because of the intense picketing, Elmer Grigsby, the company's president and board chairman, was unable to access his office through the front door. The bucket hoist that was used to enable Grigsby to enter through a third story window was withdrawn from service. As the beleaguered president entered the building from the front door, for the first time, he maintained a stoic composure, and seemed to be oblivious of the taunts and catcalls coming from the picketers.

Reverend Arthur Stanton, spokesman for the picketing group, himself a man of considerable corpulence, said that the "Fat Broads of America" would remain until this Grigsby character resign or hell freezes over, whichever comes first.

Law Offices

COSTELLO, NEARING, BREAM AND FOSTER
666 Cassius Drive
New York, N.Y.

Elmer Dexter Grigsby, 2nd
President, Chairman of the Board
The Grigsby Crowbar Corporation
New York N.Y.

Dear Elmer:

I have been in contact with the public relations firm of Castle, Peabody Associates to help us get through these difficult times. They have been successful in dealing with problems far worse than ours, and are skilled in damage control. They will move quickly to blunt the negative media that Grigsby has been subjected to.

One of their people, Marge Thompson, is available. She has performed brilliantly in the past, and was particularly effective in the Congressman Peter Sentello tomato scandal.

Although this incident was widely publicized, you may not have been aware of it. What happened had to do with the Congressman's hobby of growing tomatoes. These weren't your ordinary garden variety of tomato. These tomatoes were. at least, twice as large as normal, were without blemish, and captured the distinctive taste of a tomato at its best. The Congressman distributed these tomatoes to favored colleagues, the media, and Washington insiders. It was considered a great honor to be favored with a gift of this luscious tomato. How the Congressman was able to grow such an extraordinary tomato was a closely guarded secret. When questioned, the congressman, with a twinkle in his eye, would say that because of national security regulations, he is prevented from responding to questions.

One of Washington's leading investigative reporters was assigned to unlock this secret. What he discovered was a horrifying, bone chilling, hair rising story that defied the imagination. In the congressman's back yard were a number of robust tomato plants. Draped around the base of each plant, was a dead cat. The Congressman was using dead cats as fertilizer. It seems that the congressman was away for a week. On his return, he looked in on his garden. He noticed a dead cat draped around the base of one of the tomato plants. He also noticed the vines and tomatoes on that plant, were far healthier than the other plants. The vines were thicker and greener, and the tomatoes were already on their way to being much larger. This was a momentous discovery, and the congressman decided to keep it a secret. He, very quickly, gained a considerable reputation for growing super sized tomatoes. How he obtained the cats was a shocking revelation. Animal lovers were not satisfied with the demand that he resign. They wanted the congressman to stand trial for the gruesome account of how he acquired the cats.

When this incredible story was published, complete with photographs, all hell broke loose. The "fortunate insiders" who received these tomatoes were beside themselves with rage. Many resorted to citrate of magnesia to purge their stomachs. Petitions were quickly circulated to have the congressman recalled, and colleagues, animal rescue organizations, all demanded his immediate resignation. Marge Thompson was assigned to work with the congressman. It was a very difficult assignment. It seemed hopeless.

Marge immediately had him admitted to a sanitarium in Switzerland. This shielded him from the media and public. Then she went to work. First reports coming out stated that he was responding well to treatment. Next, that he was well aware of his terrible acts, and the pain he had caused people he loved and respected, and he was extremely remorseful.

Next report, coming from the sanitarium, said that the congressman was thinking seriously of resigning from the congress, and that he would spend the rest of his life as a missionary, going to the furthest ends of the world. Then it was reported that he had become extremely religious, spent his waking hours in prayer, and was delivering sermons every Sunday morning. Sentiment at home did a hundred and eighty degree turn. Marge felt that the situation had improved tremendously, and that he could return home. He did and went to church every Sunday, and stayed to teach a Sunday school class. He ran for re-election, and was returned to congress by a comfortable majority. Marge Thompson's job was over.

I am grateful that Marge Thompson is available at this trying time. Please advise.

Very truly yours,
Gerald R. Bream

GRIGSBY CROWBAR CORPORATION

1 Whitemarsh Circle * New York, N,Y.

Mr. Gerald Bream
Costello, Nearing, Bream and Foster
666 Cassius Drive,
New York, N.Y.

Dear Gerald:

Your letter arrived about the same time that I was relaxing with a bloody mary. Thank you very much.

Although I am impressed with Marge Thompson's credentials, I don't think I need her services, at this time. I am being peppered from many sources, with demands to resign. I have no intention of doing so. I intend to do my best to make Grigsby the proud and profitable company it was.

The sad part about all of this is that I had been thinking that it was time to step down and retire from the Grigsby organization. Since all of these problems surfaced, I can't retire. There would be the perception that I was forced out. I intend to stay on and do my best to resolve all problems and make Grigsby the fine, respected, profitable company it was before all of this happened.

We have to see it through, and it will have to be done in a logical, business-like manner. I have to do it my way. I do appreciate your concern.

Very truly yours,
Elmer

Law Offices

Costello, Nearing, Bream and Foster
666 Cassius Drive
New York, N.Y.

Mr. Elmer Dexter Grigsby, 2nd
Grigsby Crowbar Corporation
1 Whitemarsh Circle
New York, N.Y.

Dear Elmer:

I had a preliminary meeting with Ms Cindy Pringle, of the law firm Chalmers, Whitingham, and Potts. This is the law firm that is representing the four ladies, and Ms. Pringle has been assigned to litigate the suit.

We didn't get into specifics. Ms. Pringle did say that they considered forty million dollars a fair amount, considering what the ladies had been subjected to. This was a figure that was not negotiable, and this is what they would accept to have us avoid court proceedings. I told her that I considered three dollars and eighty-six cents a more realistic number. She said that she would be looking forward to presenting her clients case, in court, before a jury. I agreed and told her that I would be looking forward to seeing her in court. There was some small talk about all the rain we were having, and then she left.

I have the report from the hospital. There were just superficial bruises. We will be preparing our defense. There is the possibility that we could sue the Danny Gilbert show once we sort out who did what. Right now we're in a preliminary phase and we have to see what develops. The best that we could hope for would be an out-of-court settlement, providing the amount is reasonable. To our advantage, the women suffered bruises that heal quickly and all traces of bruises disappear. To our disadvantage would be an attempt by the plaintiffs to prove evidence of psychological problems suffered by the ladies. The opposing side would, no doubt, have psychiatrists testify in their behalf. We, in turn would have to have our expert witnesses testify otherwise. The biggest problem would be the jury. They most always bring in verdicts favorable to the "victims." They reason that corporations can well afford to ante-up the money. If it goes against us, we will have the expense of the appeal process. An out of court settlement would be to our advantage, providing, of course, the settlement would be reasonable, nothing of the order they are asking. I just hope the climate will be such that we can put all of this behind us.

I'll keep you posted, with progress reports.

Very truly yours,
Gerald

News item

ACLU Joins Suit
In Grigsby Fiasco

New York—Troubles mounted for Elmer Dexter Grigsby, 2nd, and the Grigsby Crowbar Corporation, with the announcement by the American Civil Liberties Union of its intention to participate in the forty million dollar law-suit, as a friend of the court.

With this announcement, an ACLU spokesman, at the New York office, said that their organization. decided to become involved because of possible civil rights violations.

"These women were selected because they were women, and women who happened to be overweight. They were apparently forced to participate in an action that was humiliating, degrading, and life threatening. To make matters worse, this sorry affair was publicly sanctioned by the president, Elmer Dexter Grigsby, who himself was a willing participant in this shameful episode. He, alone, is responsible for humiliating these women and putting their lives in jeopardy. In all of this, there is a question as to whether these women's constitutional rights were violated."

A spokesman for the company would not comment, since the matter was in litigation.

* * *

News Iitem

A subdued Danny Gilbert denied having a hand on the Grigsby collapsible crowbar. "I absolutely, positively, definitely did not have my hand on the crowbar, and I wasn't anywhere near it. I really don't know whose hand was on the crowbar. I was shocked when I saw the platform collapse and the women go falling in all directions. It may have seemed that I wasn't concerned, because I was reeling off one-liners. As a seasoned performer this is automatic. I was greatly relieved to learn that the ladies were ok. I understand that the matter is to be tried in court. Again, let me say, Danny Gilbert's hand was not anywhere near the crowbar."

The subdued Danny Gilbert's mood changed. He grinned broadly.

"It's About Money" Magazine

Agnes Teesedale, staff writer

An interview with Alfred A. Mitchell
Special Assistant to the President
Grigsby Crowbar Corporation

Teesedale—So, one minute your on a cruise ship, basking in the Mediterranean sunshine, and the next minute you are rushing home to deal with a company in trouble. How do you feel about that?

Mitchell—Not too bad. I only had to swim part of the way. Seriously, I would have preferred being here when this unfortunate incident happened. I don't know what contribution I could have made that would have been helpful. It saddens me that our president, Elmer Dexter Grigsby, didn't have my support when it was needed. The character of the man came through, the way he stood up to the barrage of criticism that was leveled at him. Grigsby is a very solid organization, and much of its success is due to his capable leadership.

Teesedale—Mr. Grigsby is taking a lot of heat and ridicule. The overwhelming demand is that he resign. Why hasn't he resigned?

Mitchell—Why should he? I can tell you that I have the greatest respect for him as a human being, and as an administrator. Under his leadership, Grigsby is a good, solid company. He is needed now more than ever.

Teesedale—If he does resign, will you be in line for the presidency?

Mitchell—There's no reason for him to resign. He is the president, he's needed at Grigsby, and he's going to remain president for as long as he wants. Look, there never was any organization that existed as the "Fat Broads of America." Some sleazy, trouble making opportunists came up with bullhorns, and whatever obese ladies they could round up. They positioned themselves in front of the TV cameras and screamed their stupid heads off. Mr. Grigsby couldn't even get to the front door. The lawyers had to get an injunction to keep the picketers away from the front of the building. The minute the TV cameras shut down, the bullhorns were quiet.

Teesedale—On another subject I understand that you are a delegate to the Democratic Convention, this year.

Mitchell—Yeh. I was asked, and I accepted. This will be my second convention.

Teesedale—So who do you want to see get the nomination, the Governor or the Senator?

Mitchell—Oh, I don't know. Either one of them will make a great president. I leave that stuff for the heavy hitters. I'm just looking forward to having some fun; wearing crazy hats, batting the balloons, and hollering my head off. I understand the restaurants in that town have great food. It's just nice being with a bunch of guys.

Teesedale—With all the bitter rivalry that's been going on, surely you're leaning toward one of the two candidates. Which one would you prefer, the governor or the senator?

Mitchell—Like I said, either one will make a great president. I'm sure that by convention time one will yield to the other. We will have a candidate with solid backing. I'm not concerned about it. Either one will make a great president.

Teesdale—There's no indication that either will yield to the other. Why do you think this will happen?

Mitchell—Party unity. For the good of the party, one will yield to the other,

Teesedale—Most of the delegates, in the New York delegation, seem to favor the Senator. Have you been polled? Have you been asked your preference?

Mitchell—I don't know what poll you're talking about. I haven't been asked. They're two great guys. Either one would be good for the Democratic Party.

Teesedale—In your new position, Special Assistant to the President, what exactly do you do?

Mitchell—It is a new position. Because of all this turmoil the company is experiencing, I haven't been asked to do anything specific. When things settle down I'm sure there will be areas of interest that the president will want me to deal with. It's still a bit early.

Teesedale—The man who succeeded you as Executive Vice President, how is he doing?

Mitchell—He's doing great. I liked the way he handled sales. He has a real talent for management. He is capable in every respect. When I was asked to assist the president, I was happy to see him succeed me. That office is in very capable hands. Dave Lambert will do very well. We are fortunate to have him on our side.

Teesedale—I think we covered everything. Thank you, and have fun at the convention.

Mitchell—I'm looking forward to it, and thanks much.

Chapter Four

Gert and Babe
And Connie, and Liz,
Say good-bye Grigsby
Hello show-biz

It was inevitable that the four ladies would be contacted by a theatrical agency. The Kimmel Theatrical Agency, New York's largest and most prestigious, decided to explore these four most talked about ladies, to see if there would be latent talent to put together a show. The widespread publicity they received had interested Sid Kimmel, and he decided to investigate the possibility of capitalizing on the publicity these women were getting. The results of his interviews were encouraging.

Gert Davenport had piano lessons at an early age. She wouldn't practice. To keep her interested in music, her parents switched to the clarinet. It worked. Now she often gets called to make up a combo at weddings and bar mitsvahs. She played for Sid, and he liked what he heard.

Liz Appleton sang in a church choir. Her voice was a little thin, but with some coaching, she could learn to project and be supportive.

Ruth "Babe" Richards was a diamond in the rough. She had a rich, powerful voice, and often sang solo parts in her church choir. Sid Kimmel attended her church on a Sunday to hear her. He was intrigued by the power of her voice. A real belter. It wouldn't take much to convert her to popular music. She was a real find.

Connie Hall, the fourth woman to be interviewed, did no singing. She attended church occasionally, and sang with the congregation. She had a passing interest in show business, but became interested when Sid Kimmel mentioned the rewards that could be achieved in the present climate. Her passive interest changed to outright enthusiasm.

Sid Knew that it would take hard work to mold these four women into professional entertainers. The real plus was Babe Richards. She would be the lead singer and the other three would be supportive, with occasional clarinet solos by Gert Davenport. The experience that Gert had, playing at Bar Mitsvahs and weddings enabled her to develop a real schmaltsy sound. It would take hard work, and the time frame was short. At this time, they were front page, but that could change overnight/ by some other front page story. How to position them? How to mold these four women into professional entertainers wouldn't be easy. The other problem would be the choice of music. Clearly the audience for this group would not be screaming fourteen year olds. Sid thought that for the mature audience that would be out there; oldies would be more appropriate.

Sid got the four together and outlined his proposals. The sooner they put together a show, the better. It would take hard work and dedication but the rewards could be substantial. He would start now to put together a tour across the country. The audience was out there. They had to take advantage of every opportunity. Sid asked them if they were interested. They were.

Law Offices

Costello, Nearing, Bream and Foster
666 Cassius Drive,
New York, N. Y.

Mr. Elmer Dexter Grigsby
Grigsby Crowbar Corporation
1 Whitemarsh Circle
New York, N.Y

Dear Elmer:

One of our staff brought to my attention an article that appeared in Variety magazine. It seems that the four women signed on with the Sid Kimmel Theatrical Agency. This is the largest and most respected agency in the New York area. Their act is now in rehearsal. A nation wide tour is expected to begin shortly. In fact, they expect the first show to take place in Wilmington, Delaware. This show would be a trial to iron out all the kinks that may take place, and to test acceptance by the public. From there an extended tour would begin.

Of interest to us is the reference to the litigation that is pending. The Agency is of the opinion that the lawsuit would be time consuming and interfere with the tour schedule. The tour would be far more profitable. The suit has to be argued in court, and there is no assurance that it would be successful. They are advising the ladies to have their lawyers consider an out of court settlement.

This is a tremendous break for us. There is nothing for us to do right now. A lot depends on what happens in Wilmington. If the ladies do well they will go on with their tour. If the show is a disappointment, in all probability the Kimmel Agency will cancel. It all depends on what happens in Wilmington. If it's successful, as I expect it to be, I'm sure that I will hear from their lawyer, Cindy Pringle.

We'll keep our fingers crossed and hope the ladies enjoy a huge success.

I'm enclosing the clipping.

Very truly yours,
Gerald

Wall Street Journal

Product demand lifts Grigsby to profit

Grigsby Crowbar Corp. moved to a second quarter profit on strong demand for its new line of collapsible crowbars. Considering the turmoil and adverse publicity the company experienced recently, the street was expecting a substantial loss. Credit for this good showing was the determination of company officials, who rallied the troops to disregard the bad publicity, and to have faith in the excellence of their products. Customers responded to this show of confidence and renewed orders that had been cancelled. President Elmer Dexter Grigsby attributed this fine showing to the dedicated effort of all Grigsby employees. Grigsby stock gained two and a quarter.

*   *   *

News Item

Elmer Dexter Grigsby, president of Grigsby Crowbar Corp., participated in the Antique Automobile show, now in progress in Atlanta, Georgia. He drove his newly reconstructed Stutz Bearcat over the prescribed two-mile course, amid cheers from the onlookers. He was smiling, confident, and relaxed, a marked change from the pained and harrowed look of a man who was attacked and vilified during the time following the failure on the Danny Gilbert show. His company has fully recovered, and it was a pleasure to see him enjoying his great interest, antique automobiles.

"Break a leg"

Before going to Wilmington for their premiere performance, Sid Kimmel had the four ladies moved to a theater for a dress rehearsal. When the women first appeared on stage, they were overawed by what they saw. As Babe explained afterward, looking out from the stage, it was awesome to see a sea of empty seats; the massive chandeliers reflecting a spectrum of flashing colors, and rich, decorative designs accented with gold and silver. They could imagine what it would be like to see all of the seats occupied; all focused on the stage, and expecting to be entertained by performers with the skill and talent to give them a memorable evening of theatrical pleasure. For the first time, looking out from the stage, they realized that they had to perform as professionals, and give those who would be occupying the seats, an evening to remember. The adrenalin was flowing.

Sid Kimmel was sitting in the second row, together with the Broadway people who had coached the ladies in their music and dance routines. The dress rehearsal began. The people sitting in the second row were pleased with what they saw. Being on stage, in a theater setting, made a difference. The ladies were giving this small audience a performance on a higher level than they had known before. Obviously, performing in a theater, made a big difference. They were projecting well, reaching out, making themselves heard to the very last seat in the peanut gallery. They were not interrupted once. The Broadway people saved their comments until after the rehearsal had concluded. Sid Kimmel, and his associates were highly pleased. It was hard work, time was limited, but the end result was better than they had hoped. The "Grigsby Ladies," as they would be identified, felt that they were ready. They thought of themselves as professionals.

Next Performance "Wilmington, Delaware."

Chapter Five

News Report

Governor Bob and Senator Mike
Square off in Philadelphia

Governor Bob Callahan and Senator Mike Peterson met yet again in a debate that, at times, involved bitter exchanges, and accusations of a personal nature. As the Democratic Presidential Convention nears, both candidates went at each other in a desperate attempt to achieve a break-through. At the conclusion of the debate, it was clear that neither candidate was able to perform with telling arguments in order to be declared a winner. It was a draw when they started, and a draw at the conclusion of the debate. Both candidates will go into the convention with strong support, but not enough delegates to win the coveted prize. The damage done by the bitter charges and counter charges will send a victor into a campaign with serious wounds that won't heal readily. The two candidates obviously are contemptuous of each other.

In last night's debate, Senator Peterson insisted that the time is long overdue for raising the minimum wage. The cost of living has risen, but the minimum wage has not. Workers are not able to meet even the most basic of needs; food, housing, and medical costs. Governor Bob Callahan agreed that the cost of living had increased, but he feared that increasing the minimum wage would trigger massive layoffs. Education was the answer. Education would prepare people for better jobs and better paychecks, far in excess of what is possible with minimum wage.

"Those are the words that I hear from my Republican colleagues in the senate, word for word," said Senator Mike Peterson sarcastically.

"Those are my words, word for word, and if the Republicans agree with them that's fine. I would like the nation, Republicans and Democrats to accept them as a logical solution to the problem with minimum wage. Raising the minimum wage solves nothing," shot back the governor.

"Those are the words of the Republican party. They became your words the day you came into possession of the Republican playbook," insisted Mike Peterson.

"What country is spawning your left wing ideas? What country has furnished you with a play book that would end our way of life if their left wing proposals would be adopted? Tell us Mike. You named the Republicans as my source. Name the country that is your inspiration for all of the screwy ideas as to how this great country of ours should be governed," said the governor.

"I absolutely have no reservation about naming the country that is my inspiration for proposals that I have introduced during my long tenure in the senate. You may have heard of it. The name of that country is the United States of America, and specifically, its playbook is its farsighted and inspirational constitution. The welfare of its people is my concern, and will always be my concern," said Mike Peterson looking directly at Governor Bob Callahan.

This was typical of the exchanges that took place throughout the debate. It was "no holds barred." The moderator suggested issues, and then withdrew to let them slug it out. At the conclusion, they had each argued vehemently, and, at times, with scorching accusations of a personal nature. Neither candidate could claim victory.

It was impossible to predict which candidate would prevail at the forthcoming convention. Obviously, the battle would continue well beyond the first roll-call.

Pierre Delacroix

Music Critic

Wilmington—As the audience assembled for last night's performance by the Grigsby women, I wondered how many were there as a result of all the publicity the ladies had received. I admit to being one of them. I couldn't accept the fact that these women were employed in the business world, and then suddenly and literally catapulted into page one celebrities. I was in the audience to be entertained by professional entertainers. I didn't believe that there was enough there to be able to pull it off. Boy was I wrong.

The curtain went up, and the attire of the ladies pleased me. I wasn't expecting tutus. If they were wearing tutus, I would have left immediately. I would have seen enough. What I did see were four women in ankle length sequined designer gowns, looking quite lovely. And then they went into their first number. I was immediately captivated by the rich, powerful voice of the lead singer, "Babe" Richards. Here was a voice that seemed appropriate in any field of vocal music. It was an operatic voice, the voice in a Broadway production, and the voice of an entertainer in a program such as I was witnessing. She had a versatility that was unbelievable.

The program progressed with a highly appreciative audience liking what they saw and heard. The music was very carefully chosen, reaching back as far as Irving Berlin. The theme for the night was love and romance. Women were idolized. The music of that part of the twentieth century was chosen for this program.

All was not love and romance. One of the women, Gert Davenport, played the clarinet. The program notes described her as playing Klezmer music at Bar Mitzvas and wedding. Her handling of the clarinet certainly reflected that experience. She had the ability to get emotional sounds from sadness to happiness. She could really make the clarinet talk. In one of her numbers the other three women danced a well-choreographed, spirited dance. They held hands, moved in a circle, moving their feet in an exciting rhythm.

The evening was a rousing success. We, in Wilmington, were fortunate to have been chosen for this premiere performance. Everything went well.

The audience was particularly grateful for their generosity with encores. Those, who were responsible for putting this show together, deserve full credit for the difficult task of taking four inexperienced women, and, in one night, making them seasoned entertainment professionals. Judging from the prolonged applause, the audience saw and heard exactly what I saw, and heard.

Law Offices

Costello, Nearing, Bream and Foster
666 Cassius Drive
New York, N.Y.

Elmer Dexter Grigsby, 2nd
Grigsby Crowbar Corporation
1 Whitemarsh Circle
New York, N.Y.

Dear Elmer:

After the tremendous success that the Grigsby ladies achieved in Wilmington, there was no doubt, in my mind, that Ms.Pringle would get in touch with me. Obviously, a settlement, and a withdrawal of the lawsuit, would reflect her clients' wishes. There is no way that they would want to be distracted by unpredictable litigation. The advantage has shifted to our side.

And call, she did. She thought there was a lot of ground to cover and suggested that I come to her apartment. She assured me that I would have every law office appurtenances available in any law office. I didn't think that there was much reason for a meeting. All she had to do was withdraw the suit. She countered by saying that all I had to do was to pay her clients the amount stipulated in the suit. I could see that it wasn't going to be that easy. I accepted her invitation to meet in her apartment on Eighty-eighth street.

I arrived at her apartment on time (4 P.M.), and she immediately ushered me into one end of the apartment. It was laid out like a typical law office. There was an outer desk for the receptionist, a private office, and a conference room. On the table was a dish of Hors D'oeuvres, a pitcher of water, and a glass for each of us. I said that I never expected to see a law office setting in a condo. She said that the previous owner was a Wall Street lawyer, and he insisted that whoever succeeded him in the condo, that person should be a lawyer. It was magic. She happened to be in the right place at the right time. We began to negotiate.

I told her that, because of the huge success the Grigsby women were experiencing, this lawsuit had no interest for them. Why not give them what they want. Drop the suit. She said that she was representing them as council, and there has been no change that she was aware of. Perhaps I had more information than she had. I reminded her that the ladies wouldn't want to give up their tour to appear in court. She countered by saying that there was no need for the ladies to interrupt their tour. Testimony could be taken care of with affidavits. She was also aware that the people I represent wouldn't want a lawsuit to appear on their 10K form. That's the way it went until a strange occurrence took place.

While we were talking a Siamese cat wandered into the room. He jumped up on her lap. Ms.Pringle stroked his head. She said that her cat, Lox, wasn't particularly affectionate, but, at times, liked to have his head stroked. What was strange, unbelievable really, was that I have a Siamese cat who answers to the name of "bagel." That was just the beginning. We found that we each have an extensive David Brubeck collection, and the very rare recording of Ravel's Bolero, recorded in 1952 by the Vienna Philharmonic Orchestra, Fritz Wiedenhoffenhorst conducting, (pink label). We were convinced that our meeting was divinely inspired. Cindy and I were drawn to each other in a romantic way. Looking back, this was an experience that I never, in my wildest dreams, thought could happen. We, literally, fell in love.

Despite the deep feelings we have for each other, I want to assure you that we didn't let this interfere with our duty to our clients, as lawyers. The settlement we reached was accomplished only after hard and difficult give and take. We negotiated as lawyers, determined to do the best for our clients. To make sure that the settlement arrived at was fair to both sides; lawyers from our respective firms examined the agreement. It was approved with very minor changes.

Also, I want to assure you that Grigsby was not charged for time spent with Ms. Pringle that was not strictly business. As responsible and ethical members of the bar, we scrupulously and precisely made note of the times when I ceased to represent Grigsby and became involved with Ms. Pringle in activity of a personal nature.

Ms. Pringle and I are eagerly looking forward to that day when we will be united in wedlock, and our Brubakers will be united in one enviable collection. I can tell you that our cats have already met, and very quickly established the inseparable relationships that characterize their names, "Lox and Bagel."

Very truly yours,
Gerald

Grigsby Crowbar Corporation

1 Whitemarsh Circle
New York, N.Y.

Gerald R. Bream
Costello, Nearing, Bream and Foster
666 Cassius Drive
New York, N.Y.

Dear Gerald:

My heartiest congratulations and warmest wishes for a happy and healthy future to your pussy cats, Bagel and Lox.

                                                Very truly yours,
                                                      Elmer

Chapter Six

Financial Report

Grigsby pays $ 2.5 B for Hackman Construction Company

In a Surprise move, Grigsby Crowbar Corp. announced the proposed acquisition of the Hackman Construction Company for $ 2.5 billion dollars. Stockholders of Hackman Construction will receive forty-two dollars per share. The agreement is subject to the approval of the shareholders of both companies.

What surprised Wall Street was the size of the acquisition. Grigsby made two acquisitions in the past six months, but these were relatively small companies. This one, given the size of the acquisition, is huge in comparison.

David Lambert, an official of the company gave assurances that financing was already in place. He pointed out that Grigsby, in recent months, was doing very well, The core business, crowbars, was experiencing rapid growth, and the two acquisitions were each up over 15%. Considering that they were only a part of Grigsby for a few short months, the results are amazing. Now they are quite excited about the acquisition of the Hackman Construction Company.

"This is a company, "said Lambert," that borders on work that we are doing. It's a perfect fit and we look forward to having them as part of our company. We particularly are looking forward to the real estate periphery division of Hackman. We see real prospects for growth in that area."

The street has been encouraged by the significant progress being made by Grigsby since the unfortunate failure on the Danny Gilbert show. The company has rallied and, with skill and imagination, is achieving unbelievable success. Investment analysts are taking note of the increasing number of brokerage firms putting Grigsby on their "Buy" list. Grigsby shares dropped two and an eighth. Some analysts were troubled by the size of the acquisition.

News Item

Musical Chairs At Grigsby

New York City—Elmer Dexter Grigsby, 2nd, President and Chairman of the Board of the Grigsby Crowbar Corporation, announced today that he is resigning the presidency of the company. He will, for the time being, retain his position as Chairman of the Board. Succeeding him in the presidency is the former Special Assistant to the President, Alfred A. Mitchell. He will serve as an interim president until a successor is appointed to replace David Lambert, the present Executive Vice President. At that time David Lambert will become the president. Interim President Alfred A. Mitchell will then become the special assistant to the Chairman of the board. A search is underway to find a qualified person to be appointed to the Executive Vice Presidency. At the present time, Mr. Lambert is very intensely involved with the forthcoming integration of the new company into the Grigsby organization.

Mr. Grigsby, the beleaguered president at the time of the Danny Gilbert incident, had repeatedly resisted all attempts to force his resignation. He said, at that time, that he would resign only when the company had fully recovered, and that it would once again be the fine company that it had always been, since its founding. In his opinion, the company is enjoying spectacular growth, and the future is promising. Management has the ability to take advantage of every opportunity to continue the growth and prosperity of the company.

Since the company was founded, there always was a Grigsby at the helm. With the resignation of Elmer Dexter Grigsby, 2nd, this line of succession will come to an end. Mr. Grigsby has two sons. Both of them are happily pursuing careers in the arts, and had shown no interest in entering the business field.

Meeting between David Lambert and Alfred A. Mitchell
In Mitchell's office

David—It's very important that we have a meeting of the minds as to who does what. We don't want to be in a position where we're going in different directions.

Alfred—I don't see a problem here. You do what you do, and I do what I do.

David—There is a problem. Realistically, we're both presidents. You are the interim, temporary president. As soon as we get someone to take over my office, then I'll move into the president's office. You can't have two presidents at one time. One has to make all the decisions; otherwise you risk a chaotic situation. That's something we can't afford to have.

Alfred—That's right. Then I'll stop being interim president, and I'll become a special assistant to the Chairman of the Board. You will then become the president. We all know that.

David—Sure, that's the way it's set up. But I don't want to come into the office and find that I have to undo decisions that I wouldn't approve of.

Alfred—Whoever succeeds you, as Executive Vice President, may want to make some changes from the way you ran the office. So what. I do it my way. You do it your way, and whoever succeeds you will do it his way. When the change takes place, and you become president, then you'll have your own way of doing things, and that's the way it goes. It's no big deal.

David—It is a big deal. We're getting close to filling the Executive Vice President slot. We have a man with very good credentials. There are just a few loose ends to work out and then he'll be joining the company. It's getting close. As soon as this happens you'll be with the Board, and I'll be moving into the presidency. All I'm asking is that you do nothing to complicate the change. Make no decisions. Whatever comes up, I'll take care of. To put it bluntly, I don't want to be involved with situations that I will have to straighten out.

Alfred—I don't know what decisions I'll have to make. I don't know what will come up that I, as president, will have to deal with. It doesn't make any difference whether I'm the interim or temporary president or what. If something comes up that I have to deal with, I'll deal with it.

David—I want you to talk to me before you make a decision. You're an interim president. You don't have to do anything.

Alfred—A guy comes in lugging a water cooler. So he asks me, "where do you want it?" So I tell him to go ask the Executive Vice President. Is that what you want?

David—That's exactly what I want. I want to make all decisions.

There's silence. The two men glare at each other. Alfred blinks.

Alfred—OK, you can tell the guy where to put the water cooler, and whatever else you want to do. From here on, it's in your hands.

David—You can take long vacations, play golf, or do whatever you want. I understand you're going to the Democratic Convention as a delegate.

Alfred—I'm looking forward to it.

David—Pick a good one.

Alfred—Will try.

—Meeting over—

Alfred sat in his office thinking about his situation. It is a fact that Dave had been the driving force behind the spectacular growth of the company. No argument there. And it's also a fact that the presidency is really his. No doubt about it. So it's logical to accept David's taking control of the top management post. Nothing to do about it but do as David suggested; take long vacations, and don't rock the boat.

Vacations would be a problem. If he said anything to Martha he would soon find himself traipsing around in foreign countries, visiting old, musty cathedrals, and mingling with camera lugging tourists, elbowing their way in to get a clear shot of the changing of the guards. And then there's the shopping. Must have this, and must have that. Big deal. He would rather be with a couple guys in a wooded area, trout fishing, and frying their catch over a small fire. The problem there is he doesn't know a couple guys who do trout fishing. He never fished in his life. The same goes for shooting quail or hunting deer. He never fished or hunted, and never had any desire to do so. The only event that interested him was the national political convention, He looked forward to going. He attended one other convention before and had a rip roaring good time. So he was anticipating this one. That was the situation with vacations.

Alfred decided he would just have to make the best of it until Dave takes over. There were some papers on his desk. He pushed them aside. Whatever they were, Dave would take care of them. He thought about Dave's meteoric rise from sales manager to the presidency. Elmer recognized his potential, early on. When the crowbar collapsed, and the company was in disarray from the bad publicity, it was Dave who jumped in, held meetings all over the world, and rallied employees and customers to restore confidence in Grigsby products. He, single handedly, really saved the company. And afterward, he restructured the company; made acquisitions, and broadened the base. He really did deserve the presidency.

Alfred sat there and thought about the failure of the crowbar. It shouldn't have failed. He just couldn't understand what went wrong

News item

Grigsby Crowbar Corporation
Changes Name

A company spokesman announced today, a change in the company's name. It will no longer be the Grigsby Crowbar Corporation. The new name will be Grigsby Holdings. Grigsby Crowbar will continue as a division of Grigsby Holdings. It no longer had the dominance of past years. With the acquisitions that have taken place, crowbars are a segment of the business. Other divisions will be The Grigsby Earth Moving Company. The Grigsby Construction Company, and the newly formed Grigsby Real Estate Company.

* * *

News Item

Princeton—Princeton University students of the Sophomore class, led by Jeremy G. Pistol of Sandusky, Ohio, rigged up a platform on which five students, of various weights, were standing. As Pistol explained, they proposed to increase the load, one student at a time, until the Grigsby AK43 collapsible crowbar collapsed. A newspaper reporter, covering the event, notified the Grigsby Crowbar Corporation. The company called Princeton and protested the improper use of their product. They were very much concerned about injuries that would occur if the crowbar exceeded the safety margin. University police dispersed the students and dismantled the makeshift platform. Pistol registered a protest with the University, claiming that it was a scientific project that he intended to submit for class review, and also that he was being deprived of his constitutional rights. Administrators of Princeton were not in a mood to discuss the incident. They suggested to Pistol that, perhaps he would find happiness at some other university.

The matter was very quickly resolved. Pistol would not, under any circumstances, leave Princeton.

News item

New York—Nicholas R. Thompson, president of Swedesboro Partners vehemently denied that their accumulation of five percent of Grigsby Holdings stock was the opening salvo in an attempt to take over the Grigsby Company. "The acquisition of Grigsby stock was made purely for investment purposes. I have no intention of taking over the company," said Thompson.

Knowing Nicholas Thompson's past performance in acquiring companies, this situation will bear watching. What he has done was to attract investors to assume that the company was ripe for acquisition. A spokesman for Grigsby Holdings said that, as a matter of policy, it does not comment on matters of this kind. Grigsby stock closed up one and an eighth.

* * *

Democratic Party Delegates Leave With High Hopes

From left, Sol Schreibman, Alfred Mitchell, Clyde Windrem, and James Reilly, of the New York delegation, await departure.

News Item

Melanie DuBois, president of Women's Watch of America, registered a protest regarding the small number of women in the New York delegation to the Democratic Convention. "There are many women, in responsible positions, who were passed over in the selection of delegates going to the convention from the New York area. These women are better qualified to represent New York than many of the men who were selected. We protested early on, and the selection committee continued its deplorable policy of appointing party hacks. Women's Watch of America, as a protest, can no longer be depended upon to support the Democratic ticket.

"We are not in anybody's hip pocket. We will see how the Convention develops, and will decide which party will serve our best interests at a later time," said DuBois.

* * *

News Item

Anthony Brentwood, Republican nominee for president, returned from his brief vacation, following the conclusion of the Republican Convention. He said that he was well rested and was looking forward to the campaign. "I am not concerned about who the Democrats will nominate for president. I am looking forward to the debates, and the give and take of the campaign process. One man will emerge as the victor, and I'm quite content to leave that decision to the voters. I can only tell them what my positions are on the issues that are of concern to them. I hope they will be acceptable, and they hire me for the job."

Chapter Seven

The Democratic Convention was shifting into high gear. Delegates were optimistic that this would be their year to capture the Whit House. Who the standard bearer would be was a question. The two top contenders for the nomination were locked in a bruising battle where neither of them could garner enough delegates to achieve the nomination. Their lieutenants were busy talking to delegates on the convention floor to make sure there were no defections.

Governor Bob Callahan's strategy was to position himself slightly to the left of Republican ideology. He believed that the most effective way to defeat the Republicans was to adopt the "me too, but" technique. Agree with their position on issues, but interpret these issues to make them palatable for Democratic voters. To win the election, the Governor would have to win over as many Republican voters as possible, and yet retain the support of the Democrats. It would be a high wire act, but Governor Bob Callahan was sure it would get him into the white house. He would, of course, have to be nominated by the convention. The problem was that Senator Michael Peterson was also a strong contender for the nomination.

Senator Michael Peterson had an opposite view. His philosophy was to go head to head with the Republican opponent. He would promise the voters jobs, a substantial increase in the minimum wage, and health insurance for every man, woman and child in America. He had strong union backing, but the question was, with this doctrinaire position, could he be elected? Governor Callahan maintained that if the Senator ran, he would scare off all the conservatives, and would guarantee a Republican victory.

The senator was more of a showman. He recently went into a dress shop, with a cameraman, and went from rack to rack, reading the source of manufacture labels. He picked up one garment after another and said, "made in China." Every item he picked up had a "made in China" label. At the end he said that he would, when elected president, bring those jobs back to this country and put people back to work. That would be his first priority.

The governor scoffed at this as a grandstand play. He said that the Senator had yet to tell you how he would reverse the jobs that were exported abroad. "The truth of the matter is that the Senator has no plan that would reverse the export of jobs. If he did have a plan, he would tell you."

This was a difficult situation for the Chairman of the Democratic Party, Ted Reynolds. He wanted a decision, a resolution of this problem before the voting began. What he foresaw, and wanted to avoid, was successive balloting with inconclusive results. He pleaded with the two to put aside their differences and make a decision. He even suggested that they choose by a flip of a coin. That was not acceptable to either candidate. It was obvious that there was not going to be movement on either side. Ted talked with various state delegations to get some idea as to the relative strength of the two contestants. The Senator's backing was very solid. The Governor's not so solid. Ted felt that, on succeeding ballots, the Governor's hold on his supporters could experience defections. Still, he would want to see movement before they go to the convention floor.

Ted proposed highly qualified compromise candidates, reputable, seasoned people who were party loyalists for many years, and would have been excellent choices. None of them were acceptable to Bob or Mike, although Mike could be flexible to achieve Party unity.

Ted went down to the floor to see if he could get some movement from the various delegations. He was in a very difficult situation. As Chairman of the party, he had to weld the various factions for a united front. While making his way down the aisle, he was stopped by one of the delegates, who stood directly in his path.

"I just want to congratulate you on the wonderful work you are doing as Chairman of our party," said the delegate.

"Thank you," said Ted. "I do my best." Ted looked at the badge. It read, Alfred A. Mitchell, President, Grigsby Holdings.

Ted's eyes lit up. "I am a stockholder of your company, and I'm real pleased with your progress. You seem to be growing by leaps and bounds,"

"Thank you. We do our best."

The thought came like a flash. Why not propose a successful businessman as a compromise candidate. This would be like a breath of fresh air. Nothing else had triggered movement. The advantage would be that a businessman would be beyond the factional infighting that was tearing the Party apart. A fresh face, with no political baggage, would be a welcome change.

"Come with me," said Ted.

Soon Alfred found himself in one of the back offices. Ted introduced him to two of his assistants.

"These guys are going to ask you some questions. We want to get input from delegates so we will have some feeling about issues. Just answer them as best you can. I'll check in with you later. The interrogators went right to work.

"What's your view on abortion?"

"It's OK, I guess."

"You approve?

"Whatever the government does, is OK with me."

Were you ever arrested for drunken driving?"

"No."

Where is Zimbabwe?"

"Don't know. Never heard of her."

"It's a country, not a person."

"Never heard of it."

"Were you ever audited by the IRS?"

"No."

"What's your opinion on capital Punishment?"

"Whatever the government does is OK with me."

"Do you approve of the government of North Korea?"

"I don't know anything about their government."

"How about Cuba?"

"You don't hear much about them, anymore."

"How about Iran?'

"Don't know."

"Syria?"

"Likewise. Why am I being asked all these questions?"

"We just want to get your opinion on things. It's important to us."

It's OK. Glad to help out.

Does a woman have the right to choose?"

Why not? Everybody has that right, women, men, everybody.

What I mean is if she wants to have an abortion, she just goes to her doctor and he does the job.

Oh that. I don't think she can do that.

It's her body. Shouldn't she have the right to make decisions about her own body?

I see what you mean. I guess she should, but I think abortions are illegal.

"Can you name one Supreme Court Justice."

"Not off hand. I'd have to look it up."

"What newspapers do you read?"

"We get the Times. I usually just read the sports section. Martha, she's my wife, she reads the rest."

And so it went for about an hour. The interrogators thanked Alfred, and left to report to Ted.

They told Ted that they had never come across anyone who was so poorly informed, so completely blank. Is he really the president of Grigsby?

"Yes, he's the president of Grigsby," said Ted.

"Unbelievable," said Charley, one of the interrogators,

"The only way you can run this guy would be to wrap him in the American flag and have him invoke the help of God. He's a real loser," said Kenny, the other interrogator.

"He may be an intelligent person. He would have to be to be president of a company like Grigsby. The point is, he is embarrassingly uninformed about matters that school kids know. There's no way he could be considered a candidate for president," said Charley.

As a result of the questioning, Ted realized that Alfred could not, under any circumstances, be considered as a candidate. He was clearly lacking in all aspects of a well-rounded background. Ted couldn't understand how he could be the president of a company like Grigsby Holdings. He thought there would have to be something that they must have overlooked. He still couldn't give up on the concept of a non-political, president of a company, being an acceptable compromise candidate. Ted was inclined to send Alfred back to his delegation. The thought occurred to him that there was a possibility that Alfred, for whatever reason, was faking his answers. There was a slim chance that this was what had happened. It was just inconceivable that a man could be the president of a large company, and be so ignorant of current events. He decided to hold on to Alfred to see if this could trigger movement from the Governor and Senator. If it did, he would try to find another industrialist with a broad knowledge of issue and foreign affairs.

Later that day Ted met with the Governor. He told him that he had a compromise candidate to suggest; the president of a highly successful company, the Grigsby Corporation. Unfortunately, he did very poorly when questioned by his staff. He knew very little about events occurring beyond a five-mile radius of his house, so now they were back to a stalemate. Ted suggested finding another industrialist with good, solid credentials.

The Governor thought about his situation. He objected to the other, well-qualified compromise candidates. If one of them ran, and won the presidency, in all likelihood he could get reelected. It would then be eight years before the Governor would get another opportunity to make a run for the presidency. A lot could happen in eight years. He would be eight years older. It would be better to support a sure loser. Then he would have the opportunity to challenge again in four years. He was sure that the Senator had rejected qualified compromise candidates for the same reason. He told Ted that it might not be a bad idea to run a successful industrialist. He would agree to the selection of the man he just interviewed if the Senator would.

Ted was furious. "I have suggested any number of qualified candidates as compromises, and they were all rejected. And now you accept a man who has neither the background or interest to make a run for the presidency"

"I have great respect for your management skills. I'm sure you can find a way to get him elected," said the Governor.

"It's not just the presidency. Senators and congressmen are also running, They need a strong, proven vote getter at the head of the ticket. The presidency is not for amateurs," shot back Ted.

"I agree that you need the strongest candidate you can find to head the ticket, to win in November, and get as many senators and congressmen elected as possible. I'm that man. You're the Chairman of the Party. It's up to you to work on Mike and get him to back me. I can win and he can't. You know it and he knows it. You should convince him to support me so we can really get moving. If he still refuses to co-operate then there's nothing I can do," said Bob.

Ted didn't see it that way. "It's a fact that all of Mike's senate votes were unquestionably liberal. This is a matter of record, and it's not going to influence hard core Republicans. On the other hand, I think you would have a problem keeping up with Tony Brentwood with your 'me too, but' strategy. Tony's a different breed of Republican. He's more reasoned, more issue oriented. He's not the rigid, doctrinaire Republican that you associate with the Republican Party. No way. The voter would very soon see through your 'me too, but' tactic. Why buy a cheap substitute when you can have the well accepted, national brand product for the same money. I'm sorry to say this, but I think, in my opinion, Mike would make a better run for the presidency than you would. He's a terrific campaigner, and would give Tony Brentwood a real battle."

"I can't and don't agree with you. I'm in this race to stay. I know I can win, and all I want is the backing of my party. My strategy will work. I know it will," persisted Bob.

Ted shook his head. "I didn't want to go to the convention floor for a vote. I wanted to avoid any possibility of a deadlocked convention. I hoped that we could have worked this out, but I see we can't. There's no alternative but to have this decided on the convention floor. Whoever emerges, you, Mike or a compromise candidate, will have my full support."

"Did you talk to Mike about this, about your decision to let it go to the delegates?" asked Bob.

"I did. Mike is flexible. I don't think he would accept Alfred Mitchell, after I tell him how poorly he did when questioned. There were other very qualified people who were acceptable to him, but not to you. He won't understand why Mitchell would be seriously considered. He'd much rather have it go to the convention floor. It's really up to the delegates to make this decision, regardless of how many roll calls it takes. He won't release his delegates to you. He is confidant that, going head to head on the first roll call, he'll get more votes than you will. He might not make it on the first roll call, but he is certain your support is soft and from then on will erode. He's sure he'd go over on the next roll call. He does have a solid base, and I think he could do well with the delegates," said Ted

"I'm not concerned about the outcome, if it goes to the floor. However, in the interest of party unity; I agree to the acceptance of this industrialist fellow, whatshisname. If it goes to the floor, and Mike wins, I just don't know. I am a party loyalist, but with Mike at the head of the ticket, I'd have to consider my options," said Bob.

Ted's first thought was to submit his resignation. There is no way he could go along with sheer insanity. On second thought, he could not resign. The rank and file, running for office, depended on him. Another option was to ignore the Governor; take it to the floor of the Convention, and let the delegates decide. Ted was sure the senator would get the nomination. What he wasn't sure of was the Governor's reaction. What would he do during the campaign? Would he bolt to the Republican side? Would he form a third party? Would he just sit it out? Would he do what he could to get the Senator elected? Ted didn't trust the Governor. He didn't want to go into the election with a party in disarray.

Ted went back to talk to Mike, and to report his conversation with Bob. Mike was livid.

"For the sake of party unity, I was willing to accept any of the highly qualified compromise candidates you suggested. None were acceptable to him. And now he agrees to this Mitchell fellow. This is outrageous. The only way to go is to let the delegates decide. I'm sure I can win. At the very worst, I can block him, and you can then propose a qualified compromise candidate. No way will Bob get the nomination, and certainly we don't want Mitchell. That would be courting disaster."

Ted agreed that Mitchell would be a very poor choice. It would take a lot of hard work to bring him up to speed. The problem was Bob. If it went to the floor, and Bob lost, how would he react? He certainly wouldn't be a gracious loser and wholeheartedly support the winner. Would he run as a third party candidate? Would he take his conservative supporters and join forces with the Republicans? Why was Mitchell acceptable to him? What surprises does Bob have that Ted hadn't thought about? Certainly, the acceptance of Mitchell was a big surprise.

Ted and Mike discussed the problem at great length. Although Mike would have preferred to go head to head with the Governor, and slug it out on the convention floor, he was sympathetic to Ted's concerns. Mitchell was Bob's choice. The hope was that Bob would be loyal to the Party during the campaign.

Ted couldn't put it off. He had to have a talk with that "industrial fellow, whatsisname."

Chapter Eight

Ted would have preferred a seasoned, well-qualified candidate for the top of the ticket Alfred A. Mitchell would barely qualify in a race for water commissioner, but in a clash of wills between two rival contestants, this is how it was resolved. Alfred A. Mitchell would be the choice of the Democratic Party Convention. The only plus that Ted could see, was personality. Alfred, on first contact, seemed pleasant and likeable. The big problem was to somehow impart the vast amount of basic knowledge that any candidate for president is expected to know. For Alfred this would be a difficult transformation. For Ted it would be a monumental challenge. Alfred would have to look like a candidate, talk like a candidate, and think like a candidate. Time was a problem. Ted went right to work. First, Alfred should be informed.

Ted took Alfred into his office. "It's been decided. You're going to get the nomination for president."

Alfred was puzzled. "Why would I get the nomination? I'm not running for anything. I wouldn't know what to do. This is some mistake. You better get somebody else."

Ted explained. "We did try to get somebody else. Senator Michael Peterson wanted the nomination, and so did Governor Robert Callahan. Neither of them had enough backing to win, so they decided to back a compromise candidate. They chose you."

"I don't know them. They don't know me. It doesn't make sense. I don't know what this is all about. I'm sorry. I'm just not interested. I don't want to do something I couldn't do," said Alfred.

"They know that you're the president of Grigsby Holdings, a very prestigious company. They felt that an industrialist, who is non-political, would be the best choice for president. I agree," said Ted.

Alfred could see the problem. It was Dave Lambert who, single handedly, achieved the spectacular growth of the company. It was Dave Lambert who saved the company after the Danny Gilbert disaster. Ted did not know that he had only been president a very short time, just a very few days, really, and he had not made any contribution to the growth of the company. In fact, he was a toothless tiger. He wasn't even permitted to tell the guy where to put the water cooler. It was a case of mistaken identity. On the basis of achievement, Dave Lambert should be offered the presidential nomination, not him. How could he explain all of this to Ted? It would be difficult. Yet, Ted must be told. Ted had to know why it would be impossible for him to be considered for the presidential nomination.

Alfred did try to explain his situation to Ted, that others were involved in the growth of the company. He had very little to do with it. Ted thought Alfred was being very modest, self-effacing; that he did not want to take credit for the good things that happened at Grigsby. After fruitless attempt to convince Ted that he was in no way qualified, Alfred, reluctantly, and still thoroughly confused, capitulated. When Ted said that it was his patriotic duty to accept the nomination. That did it. If it came down to a matter of patriotism, how could he not agree to run for president?

The problem was massive. Although Alfred was the president of a thriving corporation, he had none of the sophistication or well rounded knowledge usually associated with presidents of corporations. The sad part was that Alfred was well aware of being a bush league player in a big league ballpark. He would have been happy, and very much relieved, if he had been sent back to his New York delegation to swat balloons and wear funny hats. He was trapped by the turn of events, as was Ted Reynolds.

Ted talked with Alfred. He told him what to expect during the coming week. There will be many speeches by party notables. Ted suggested that he could relax and see and hear the speakers on a monitor in the comfort of living quarters, reserved for the presidential candidates.

"This will give you a good idea about what's going on, in our country and around the world, how it affects us, and what we, as Democrats, should do about it. Between speeches there will be commentators who will give their opinion about the speeches they heard, and the significance of the speeches," said Ted.

Alfred was petrified. "I can't spend all day listening to speeches, or people talking about what they heard the speaker say. I won't remember anything, because I won't know what they're talking about. I'm really not interested. I can't do it. I just can't."

Ted tried to be reassuring. "All you have to do is listen to the speeches and the commentary. If you don't remember anything, it's no big deal. Nobody's going to grade you on what you remember. There are no test papers involved. I'm asking you to do this because some of it will register on your sub-conscious. You don't have to concentrate on what is being said, or who said what. All I'm suggesting is that you expose yourself to what is being said. You can sit there sipping a cola, and munching peanuts. If a smattering of what is said rubs off, we're that much to the good, and it will help with the campaigning. I can guarantee that. Trust me."

"I trust you, Ted, but all of this is new to me, and I know I can't do what you expect of me. I don't know how the hell I can learn all I have to learn to run in this campaign."

Ted smiled. "You may not believe this, but you have already learned a lot more than you think you have. You're well on your way to being able to do the job we know you can do. If you relax and let us guide you through, you'll do OK. As the Chairman of the Democratic Party, my job is to get guys elected. That's what it's all about."

Alfred shook his head. "I came here as a delegate. All I expected, and wanted, was to be a part of the crowd. All I expected was to do a little hollering, to be a part of the convention with balloons, confetti, to wave signs, and just to be one of the guys. And now you tell me I'm going to be the candidate. I don't know what's going on or how it happened. I'm not political"

"That's why you're going to be the candidate. You're going to be the candidate, because you're not political, you're not the kind of guy who spends all his time trying to round up delegates to vote for him. You're not the kind of guy who is pompous and egotistical. You are, by nature, unassuming and reserved. These are qualities not possessed by the average politician. We think that it's time to give the voters the opportunity to consider a man who has accomplished much in the business world, yet with true humility.

Alfred was puzzled by Ted's inability to understand that he really hadn't accomplished much in the business world. He tried to get Ted to understand this, but to no avail. Ted believed only what he wanted to believe. He was the president of a thriving corporation. He wasn't concerned about details.

There was no arguing with Ted. Alfred would have to go along, do what he would be told to do, and try to do the best that he could. He finally was resigned to a situation not of his choosing. Then, the inevitable happened. The new developments were leaked to the press. From now on there was no turning back. From coast to coast, the news was out. Alfred A. Mitchell, president of Grigsby Holdings, would be the choice of the Democratic Party. This was a very unusual strategic move. "It will be interesting to see if a man, with no political background, can maneuver through the grueling minefields of a political campaign for the highest office in the land." This was the opinion of many of the editorial writers commenting on the very unusual choice of the Democratic Party.

News item.

Demos To Run Industrialist For President

Alfred A. Mitchell, President of Grigsby Holdings,
Slated For Top Spot On Ticket

In a surprise move, it was learned that Alfred A. Mitchell, President of Grigsby Holdings, will be nominated for the presidency. A source, which did not wish to be identified, said that there was agreement, by the two major contenders, to support the industrialist, Alfred A. Mitchell. Senator Michael Peterson, who was locked in a bitter battle with Governor Robert Callahan for the nomination said. "It became apparent that one of us would have to yield to the other in order to break the stalemate. Neither of us was willing to do so. The only way we could get movement was to agree to a compromise candidate. Alfred A. Mitchell was chosen because Grigsby Holdings, under his presidency, had achieved remarkable growth. Also, he is non political, and it was felt that he could attract voters of both persuasions, Republican and Democratic. For the sake of party unity, this was a wise choice."

Officials of the Democratic Party were grateful that the two contenders, Senator Michael Peterson and Governor Robert Callahan were willing, for the good of the party, to release their delegates, and recommend support for the industrialist, Alfred A. Mitchell. By doing this they avoided a bitter battle that would split the party. By uniting behind Mitchell, there was a strong indication that the Democrats were going to stress efficiency and a business-like approach to government.

Republican candidate Tony Brentwood was asked what he thought of this very unusual development.

"A man who has had a distinguished career in the business community should do well in this campaign. I'm sure he will be attractive to many voters. He may even get enough votes to finish second."

Alfred running for president?

You gotta be kidding!

Back at the Grigsby offices there was disbelief. How could Alfred get to be the standard bearer of the Democratic Party? It was as though he had the winning ticket and won a zillion dollars in a lottery. The man went to the convention to eat good food and have some fun with the guys. Aside this amazing news was concern as to how it would affect the company. David Lambert hastily called a meeting with Ralph Esposito, Bob Benton, Elmer Grigsby, and Jerry Silverman (who was induced to rejoin the company). David suggested that it would be helpful to remove the word "interim" from Alfred's title. They should help him in every way that they could. Elmer agreed and said that he would take care of it. Of major concern was the paper trail Alfred left behind. If the press should come into possession of these memos, it could be very damaging to Alfred's campaign. It probably would affect the company, although to a lesser extent. The suggestion was made that they probably should be collected and destroyed. Jerry didn't think it should be done. He wasn't sure about legal involvements, but if, in some way, these memos were needed as evidence, there could be serious problems. The decision was to ignore the memos, and just hope that they wouldn't come to light.

Another problem. They were being swamped with congratulatory messages. How do you deal with that? Also, media people wanted interviews that would shed some light on their new, emerging celebrity. There's always was the possibility that something unexpected would surface and have to be dealt with. All eyes focused on Jerry who, among the group, would be able to cope with this new situation. Jerry grimaced, but said that he would do what he could to help Alfred. They were well aware of the struggle going on between the two front-runners, the Senator and the Governor. They expected one to emerge from the rivalry, and they would all unite behind him. They were certain that when Alfred left, in his mind being chosen the democratic candidate was inconceivable. It never would have occurred to him. News reports had him identified as a compromise candidate. What credentials could he possibly have had to be chosen as a candidate for the highest office in the land? Even if, by some unusual set of circumstances, the candidacy was offered to him, it would be inconceivable that he would accept.

The meeting broke up with a lot of head shaking. It was just beyond belief that the man they knew so well could become the Democratic Party standard bearer. It just didn't make sense. There just wasn't any logic to this choice. It just didn't add up. What did the party kingmakers know that they didn't know?

One man felt the same way. Alfred A. Mitchell.

One word describes Alfred at this time.

"Bewildered"

Chapter Nine

Alfred sat there with the look of a prizefighter who had just gone through eleven grueling rounds, and who knew they would push him off the stool for a punishing twelfth. He just wanted to be left alone. Congratulatory well wishers kept coming in; chairmen of the various state delegations, politicians, a hair dresser who did things with his hair, and some lady who did things with his face. And then there were photographers who insisted that he smile, turn this way, and that way. They told him that he would be the Democratic candidate for President. What the hell. Nobody told him that they wanted him to have the nomination. He never told anyone he wanted the nomination. He never even thought about it. He was just getting pushed around. He was being manipulated.

And then, out of nowhere, there was Martha. How the hell did she get here so fast? She fell all over him. "I'm so proud," she said. Then she started to bawl. This upset the lady who had been doing things to her face.

"You are not allowed to cry. Your tears are ruining your make-up. Now I have to do it all over again. I'm getting you in shape for the photographers."

"I can't help it," said Martha. "I'm just so proud."

The make-up lady eyed the ceiling, in disgust, and then went to work on Martha's face.

And then there were his two daughters. Out of nowhere they came bouncing in. They're supposed to be in school.

"Daddy, Oh Daddy, guess what. All the kids in school wanted my autograph." said Liz, the older one. "Hi Daddy," said Patty, the younger one. "You have make-up on your face."

The Mitchell family was assembled for a family photo session. In this series of photographs, Martha was composed. It probably was because she was busy being a mother.

"You shouldn't have come here wearing those torn dungarees," said Martha to Patty.

"That's how they sell them, Mom. They tear them at the factory."

The behind the scenes activity was at a high level. There was so much going on in preparation for the big day. In one office, writers were busy writing speeches. The big one would be Alfred graciously accepting the presidential nomination of the Democratic Party.

"This is a tough assignment. The guy never smiles. He acts like he's doing you a favor by accepting the nomination. I don't know how to get this dead fish fired up so we can get some mileage out of the speech. I don't know what they were thinking of when they zeroed in on him."

"The tough part is the delivery. He's going to have to learn how to use the prompter, and time is short. I don't know how it can be done. He's a slow learner."

"Our job is to get the damned thing written. What happens afterward is their problem. He's their boy. They'll have to deal with him. What we have to do is have a talk with him. We have to find out where the log cabin he was born in is located. We'll also have to find out what he did with the money he earned cutting grass and delivering newspapers."

"What will help is if we keep in mind that the Democratic candidate is really the Republican candidate. It will make it a lot easier for us. Tony Brentwood has charisma. Alfred Mitchell is about as charming as a smelly sneaker."

"Yeh, there's this story that when Ike Eisenhauer was finishing off his first term and he got an attack of some stomach thing.

"It was illiitis."

"Whatever, the question came up, would he be well enough to run for a second term? The answer was, "we'll run him if we have to run him stuffed."

"Did they run him stuffed?"

"I don't think Adlai Stevenson ever did find out, stuffed or unstuffed. He couldn't lay a glove on the charismatic war hero."

"I come across Adlai's name in crossword puzzles. It's usually, Ike's opponent in 1952."

"Do you think this Mitchell guy is stuffed?"

"No, I think, from my observation, that he's petrified. He's scared silly. My sixth sense tells me that he really doesn't want the nomination. He was talked into it. How, or why, I don't know. I thought it would be either Bob or Mike. I guess Ted couldn't get one to yield to the other. This Mitchell guy is a strange kind of compromise candidate."

"I don't know why he would want it. He's president of a prestigious company, and I'm sure he's enjoying a big salary, bonuses, and generous stock options. Why should he give up all of that for a job that he may or may not get, and for which he has to go through a tough campaign. If he succeeds, the pay isn't that great, and who needs the aggravation. I can understand why he has that unhappy look.

"Plus the retirement package. That's when they really rake in the big bucks."

"So why are we sitting here, wasting our time writing speeches, when we could be in private industry raking in the big bucks."

"We have the wrong degrees. We should have MBA's. When you major in nineteenth century literature, you wind up writing speeches for professional politicians.

"We haven't started on Mitchell's acceptance speech yet, but I know, already, what the first words of it will be."

"What are they?"

"You know that after the candidate is introduced, he comes to the podium and wild cheering breaks out, and lasts for about fifteen minutes. He nods, looks real pleased, and acknowledges this show of enthusiasm. Then when the manager thinks that it has gone on long enough, he nudges him, and the candidate turns to the right and says 'thank you,' then he turns to the left and says 'thank you."

"So, I don't get it."

"Thank you,' they are the first words of his acceptance speech."

"Very profound observation."

"I thought so."

"You may have something there. Suppose we have him say; thank you, thank you, thank you for about an hour, and then have him say, simply,' I accept the nomination' I think we have the acceptance speech finished."

"It makes sense, but they won't buy it. We better get started. It's going to be rough going."

Outside the offices, on a long table, sample posters were being considered. One poster said Win Mit Mitchell. Time was short. The printer was waiting patiently for a decision.

"I think it's catchy, different. It may just work."

"I don't know. Isn't 'mit' a German word? I don't think it's worth the risk of being misunderstood. I think it should be simple and direct. Let's be on the safe side. Let's just say 'Win With Mitchell.' That should do it."

"I guess you're right. They have to be delivered to the delegates. The sooner the better."

At this point, Democratic Chairman Ted Reynolds thought it would be advisable to have a quiet chat with Alfred, away from all the intense activity that was going on at this time. The two sat down in Ted's office.

"If you have a feeling like Alice had when she was in Wonderland, I wouldn't be surprised," said Ted. "I know all of this is strange to you."

"More than strange. I can't understand what you want, why I'm here. I don't know what this is all about, and what you want me to do." said Alfred.

"That's OK. I can understand how you feel. We don't want you to do anything you don't want to do, and we do understand how this whole business can be overwhelming. From our point of view, we have to be sensitive to what people want. Professional politicians turn off voters. They want a fresh face. Our research indicates that they will respond to someone who isn't a politician, but one who has had a successful career outside of government," said Ted.

"There are companies out there, much larger than Grigsby. You can choose a president with a lot more experience than I have had."

"We could," said Ted," I'm sure we could have selected someone with great credentials, who would be proud to devote his time and energy to the needs of the country he loves. The truth is we have found that person. You were civic minded to take time off from your presidential duties to come here as a delegate, to help mold a future for our party, and our country. We are grateful for that sacrifice. We are now asking you, for love of country, to campaign across this nation, and lead us to victory in the fall election. It's asking a lot, but I know you can do it."

Alfred threw up his hands. He didn't know what to say. Everyone was looking to him to do what he hadn't the slightest idea what to do, or how to do it. And now it was his patriotic duty, for love of country, to be the candidate for the President of the United States, and perhaps President of the United States. The man sitting opposite him was the Chairman of the Democratic Party. Couldn't he see that he didn't know what they would expect him to know? Sure he read a newspaper, sort of, mostly the sports pages. The best use he made of a newspaper was to roll it up and swat flies.

"If it's my patriotic duty to do it, then I'll do it. I don't know beans about this whole business. I love this country. I think God has been good to us, and it's great being an American, but you picked the wrong guy. You're going to have to tell me what to do every step of the way."

"There hasn't been a president since George Washington who wasn't surrounded by very capable advisors, knowledgeable people in every field, to help and advise the president on every conceivable issue. When you become president, you will have advisors who know government and would be with you every step of the way. If you were the kind of person who would make decisions on your own, that would be a dictatorship. We don't want a dictator, right?"

"Oh no, of course not. I just didn't understand. I was afraid I wouldn't know what to do."

"It's a team effort, and you're an important member of the team. We're getting ready to play hard ball with the Republicans. The winner gets to run the country for the next four years. We think we can do a better job than they can. You can get in there, with all of us with you, and show the Republicans that they have a real battle on their hands. We're all set to go. Are you ready and willing to get in with your team-mates and help us win?"

Alfred looked at Ted. After all of that, how could he not be a member of the team? "I still don't know why you want me to run for president. It's such a big job. But I'll do whatever you want."

Ted had a broad grin on his face. "You told me what I want to hear. I'm more convinced now that we have the right man. We will be with you all the way."

Ted got up and extended hi hand to Alfred. "I am shaking the hand of the next President of the United States."

Alfred smiled. It was the first time Alfred had smiled without being told to say "cheese."

"We took the liberty of moving you to a new suite of rooms. They are more suitable for a man who is going to be the next president of the United States. Martha and the children are already there." Ted led Alfred down the corridor and stopped in front of a door. "This is where you'll be living for the rest of the week.

The rest of the week was truly Alice in wonderland. Alfred experienced the proceedings, an endless number of speeches, some of them rallying the faithful to work hard to defeat the Republicans who would, if they should win the election, make the rich richer, and the poor poorer. And then there was the business of getting candidates nominated, the election procedure, the voting by the states, the declared winner, the acceptance speech, the election of the vice President, and the business of the convention having been completed the Democrats disperse to do battle with the Republicans.

It was a busy week for Alfred. Ted Reynolds kept him informed as to what was going on, and the significance of what was going on. Various "favorite sons were honored by having their names placed in nomination. Ted explained that it was a way of giving them recognition, and that they would withdraw later. Congressman Porter Draper Jones, a gifted orator, was recruited to place Alfred's name in nomination. Listening to this Congressman, you could close your eyes and swear you were hearing Winston Churchill.

{Excerpts)

"I have made many speeches in my lifetime, but I gotta tell you, I feel honored to have been chosen to place this name in nomination. This is a man who is destined to take his place in history as one of the great presidents of all time."

(Applause)

This is a man who has all of the qualifications to achieve greatness in the presidency, and yet is modest and reluctant to speak of his past accomplishments. I gotta tell you, in the world of business, he demonstrated an ability to achieve results in the spectacular growth of his company.

(Applause)

What he did for business, he'll do for this great country of ours.

(Applause)

This is a religious man. He believes in God. He's in church every Sunday, rain or shine.

(Applause)

I gotta tell you. He's a real man. He doesn't sit down to put on his pants.

(Applause)

He puts them on, one leg at a time.

(Applause, laughter)

No matter how busy he is, I gotta tell you, he always has time to brush his teeth twice a day.

(Applause)

He's a family man. He's devoted to his wife and children.

(Applause)

This is a man who believes wholeheartedly in the quotation from the bible, "Love thy neighbor as thyself."

(Applause)

I gotta tell you. This is a man who can walk and chew gum at the same time.

(Applause)

This is a man who shovels the snow off the sidewalk of his neighbor, an elderly widow.

(Applause)

And I gotta tell you. This is a man who is anxious to get going, to go out and talk with voters all over this great country of ours.

(Applause)

He loves the United States of America. He'll work hard to preserve its great traditions. I gotta tell you, he's determined to make it the best place on earth to live, to work, and to enjoy life.

(Applause)

I gotta tell you.

(Applause)

I gotta tell you. This is a man who eats prunes with his breakfast, every morning.

(Applause}

It is my extreme pleasure to be here, to nominate the next president of the United States of America, Alfred . . . Avery . . . Mitchell.

(Sustained Applause)

Alfred and Ted watched the nominating speech by Congressman Jones on the monitor.

"Porter did very well, as I knew he would. He really had the delegates fired up,' said Ted.

"He sure did," agreed Alfred.

"No question, you'll be nominated on the first ballot."

At this stage, a significant change occurred. Alfred no longer thought of himself in terms of inadequacy and self-doubt. He no longer thought of being president as an objective far beyond his capabilities. He now accepted his assignment as the presidential candidate. He was part of a vast organization with one objective, to win control of the government. His role was to be a part of the team with the determination to win the election in November. What triggered the transition was the realization that he was not involved in initiating strategic planning or tactics to be used. This was the job of the seasoned politicians. Speechwriters furnished him with scripts. All he had to do was read them. He was beginning to feel the excitement engendered by the competition with the Republicans. They were the bad guys. They had to be defeated at all costs. Their philosophy of government would be a disaster for the average working guy and disadvantaged people across the country. Alfred was determined to work hard to prevent this from happening. What was significant in the transition was that Alfred had no responsibility for initiating programs or fielding problems that could arise. This was the responsibility of Ted Reynolds, Chairman of the Democratic Party and his assistants. With their support, Alfred could concentrate on the job of finding favor with the people he hoped would vote for him.

So it was, the next day, Alfred watched the voting on the monitor. He had been assured that the votes were committed to him, and that he would win handily. And so it went, from Alabama, the first state called, and in alphabetical order, the succeeding states. One after another responded, preceded by some flowery description of their state, with all votes cast for Alfred. It had been previously arranged that the number of delegate votes needed to win, would be cast by the State of New York, Alfred's home state. And that is the way it happened. With the vote by the State of New York, Alfred A. Mitchell was the presidential nominee of the convention.

With New York's winning vote, the convention broke into wild demonstrations. The aisles were soon filled with happy delegates waving banners, batting balloons and responding joyfully to the band playing "Happy days are here again." After, a smiling Alfred, with Martha and daughters Liz and Patty, ascended the podium. Patty was not wearing the stylishly, torn dungarees. She was tastefully dressed. Martha had seen to that. The family acknowledged the wild cheering of the delegates. After about ten minutes, they were ushered off the stage, waving to the delegates as they left. Alfred had work to do. He had to read over, and familiarize himself with the acceptance speech that was handed to him.

The next day, and Alfred was at the podium to deliver his acceptance speech. Reading it, the night before, he was amazed to find incidents in his life that were, in his mind, vague and not clearly defined. Some references in the speech were completely unfamiliar. Yet, how they were able to do this, in so short a time, was incredible. The speechwriters did a remarkable job in putting all of this together. He was coached on how to read the speech as effectively as possible.

The greeting he received was as expected; noisy, enthusiastic, and thrilling. The band kept playing, ignoring the speaker's attempt for quiet, so he could get into his speech. A broadly smiling Alfred turned to the right and said "Thank you." Then he turned to the left and said "Thank you, thank you very much." This went on several minutes, and then, on cue, there was silence, and Alfred read his speech.

(Excerpts)
In the mid nineteenth century, my great grandfather came to this great country, to live a better life, to be a part of a fast growing democracy, and last, but not least, to find and marry one of the local young ladies. He was nineteen, at the time, and arrived without a nickel in his pocket.

(Applause)

He went to work as a helper to a blacksmith. Eventually he opened his own shop, and, in his lifetime, he shoed many a horse. He survived many a kick from a horse that didn't exactly approve of what was being done to him.

(Applause)

Today, blacksmiths are rare, as are the work-horses.

(Applause)

My grandfather, too, spent his work years with horses. He was a milkman. He worked for a dairy, and, with a horse and wagon, delivered milk to his customers. That horse knew the route as well as my grandfather. He would move up as my grandfather delivered the milk. The only problem was when they got to the last house that horse would be anxious to get back to the stable, and would take off like a shot. My grandfather would always tether the horse, or have someone hold the reins while he made his last delivery.

(Applause)

Today, the delivery-man is history. Today you go to the super-market for milk or whatever else you need. The story of America is one of constant change. The story of the Democratic Party is that we anticipate the need to adapt to changes, for the betterment of our people, for the betterment of people everywhere.

(Applause)

The other party, I'm sorry to say, consider changes only to benefit the elite few.

(Applause)

The other party devises tax breaks to benefit the elite few.

(Applause)

The other party completely ignores the needs of working people.

(Applause)

Let me tell you about the other party. They completely ignore the needs of all of the poor people of the United States of America, universal health care, minimum wage and housing that is affordable

(Applause)

Let me correct something I just said. The other party didn't ignore the poor people in our land. They increased their numbers.

(Applause)

You know the story of the other party. The rich get richer and the poor get poorer. And, if there is any doubt in your mind as to the identity of the other party, I'll tell you. They call themselves Republicans.

(Applause)

We are not here to criticize all Republicans. I am hopeful that when we go to the polls, many will agree with our agenda, and support us in November.

(Applause)

We listen to the voice of the people. We hear what you are saying, what you think government should be doing, what your needs are, and what our worldwide responsibilities are. And above all, we want the good life for every man, woman, and child in America.

(Applause}

We are going to take our message, the many wonderful proposals that were made at this convention, to every part of this wonderful country of ours. We're going to tell the people that this is what we believe, and ask for their support.

(Applause)

We are going to make sure that everyone understands that security is a first priority, and we will do all in our power to assure the safety of all of our citizens.

(Applause)

Once again, we are going to have a society built not on what you have, but who you are.

(Applause)

Once again, manufacturers; all over this great land of ours, will be proudly using labels that say "Made in The United States of America."

(Applause)

I tell you again and again, we are dedicated to do everything in our power to restore faith in government, hope for a bright future for every, man, woman and child in America.

(Applause)

We can do it. We will do it. We must do it.

(Applause)

With your help, with your dedication, with your enthusiasm,

(Applause)

With your active participation, holding hands clear across this wonderful nation of ours, we will prevail in November. We will be victorious. We will win.

(Applause)

We will once again have a responsible government in Washington, dedicated to serving the needs of all our people.

(Applause)

God bless all of you. God bless the United States of America. God bless all of our Military, wherever they are, around the world. Thank you for giving me the opportunity to carry your message of peace, good health and prosperity to all of our people.

(Sustained applause)

The band came alive with the playing of "Happy days are here again," hundred of placards were enthusiastically waved, balloons descended from the rafters, and the noise level was at a peak with the yelling of the delegates. A smiling Alfred was at the podium, acknowledging the enthusiastic response to his acceptance speech. Martha and the children, all holding hands, joined him.

Ted Reynolds congratulated Alfred on his splendid delivery. Ted was real pleased with the change. This Alfred seemed more confident in his role as the presidential candidate. He was smiling easily, and seemed to be enjoying the spotlight. He had made great strides toward emerging as a creditable standard bearer of his party.

Congressman James Rockwell of South Carolina agreed to accept the vice presidency. Since Alfred was from New York, they needed a southerner to balance the ticket. Congressman Rockwell was well known throughout the south, and very well regarded by colleagues and the community at large. After Congressman James Rockwell's nomination for Vice President, they all assembled on the podium, the two families, Mitchell's and Rockwell's, clasping hands and acknowledging the sustained applause of the delegates.

With no more business to transact, the Democratic Convention was declared ended.

Did the guys back at Grigsby watch the convention?

That they did!

They were glued to their TV sets, and they were amazed at what they saw. This man they watched was a totally different person than the Alfred Mitchell they knew so well, or thought they knew so well. This Alfred Mitchell was completely in control and came off with statesmanlike qualities. He was, in every respect, a man who measured up to the attributes one would expect of a candidate for the highest office in the land. He came off as a totally different person than the one that was told that he would not be permitted to tell the man where to put the water cooler.

No one could explain the dramatic change from what they knew to what they saw. Ralph Esposito tried. He thought that what they saw was not the Alfred Mitchell they knew. What they saw was a life-size toy replica of Alfred. It had a key in the back, and when wound, it was programmed to look and talk like a gifted politician, and that's what we saw and heard during the week.

"That could be," said David. "They probably have Alfred tied and gagged in the basement."

Jerry Silverman said he was swamped with messages of all kinds. He had a ton of requests from every conceivable organization to provide speakers for specific occasions He really needed to expand his staff to be able to handle the volume, but was reluctant to do so. He was concerned about the inter-office memos. Someone could get access to them and leak them to the press. It would be better to work within his department, as it was now constituted. Jerry made use of form letters to blunt the incoming mail where a reply would be indicated. Also, a form letter was used to explain the reason why speakers from the company would not be available. "Although we are very proud to have one of our own a candidate for president, it is an election that is contested by multiple parties, and, as a matter of policy, Grigsby Holdings does not get involved in political matters."

Elmer was as confused, as was the others. He had known Alfred back to the time when he caddied for him. He thought he knew him very well. He was very much impressed with the dramatic change. There was no way he could explain it. The thought occurred to him that if Alfred should lose the election and decide to return to Grigsby, how could he position him? It would be much easier if Alfred won the election.

Over and above Alfred's situation as a candidate for the presidency of the United States of America, he had attained celebrity status. He was now well known in every corner of the Union. Being a celebrity made a big difference. Grigsby was the place where he used to work.

Chapter Ten

News Item

No Agreement,
No Debates

The Democrats and Republicans met to discuss the format for the traditional debates. The Democrats were well aware that Alfred was no match for the Republican choice for president, Anthony "Tony" Brentwood, the former attorney general. The Republicans suggested that the debates take place, as they have in previous years. It worked well so why change. The Democrats thought it was time for a change. They thought that it was a mistake to have the debates in a theater type setting. Also, they would eliminate a live audience. They suggested that the debates take place in a conference room setting. Present would be the two presidential contenders. Also present would be two advisors on each side. The candidates and/or the advisors would answer questions. By having the debates as they proposed, the voters would get information that was totally accurate.

The Republicans scoffed at this proposal. They insisted on having the debates with the format that had always worked well in the past. The Democrats would not budge from their position. They knew that Alfred would be totally destroyed by Tony Brentwood. No way would the Party permit this to happen. The Republicans were aware of this, and they went through the negotiating procedure knowing that the Democrats had no intention of exposing their candidate to Tony Brentwood, a gifted speaker and possessor of a broad background in both domestic and foreign affairs.

It was a match up that the Republicans had hoped for, but no way would the Democrats permit it to happen.

So the media was informed that the two parties were unable to agree on the format of the debates. For this election, there would be no debates. It was obvious to the media that an industrialist, with no previous experience in political give and take, would be at an extreme disadvantage in a debate with the Republican candidate. Media, with a Republican orientation, was contemptuous of the Democrats for refusing to expose their candidate to the debates. Others recognized the problem, and they understood that there was something to be said for the Democratic argument. At any rate, debates were out for this campaign.

The Mitchell strategy was simple. First, get out there and shake as many hands as possible. Second, as you shake a hand, look the person in the eye and say, "God bless you." Or say, "I love the United States of America." Alfred A. Mitchell did exactly that. Of course there were times when some enterprising reporter shook hands, accepted the blessing, and then asked a question.

Question: Mr. Mitchell, what would you do to get the budget balanced?

Mitchell: That's a very good question. What would I do to get a balanced budget? No problem. I would go back to the last time the budget was balanced. I would get a copy of that budget, take it to a super market, throw it on a scale and make a note of how many pounds and ounces it weighed. I would then notify congress that any budget weighing above this amount would be immediately vetoed. Congress would understand that there would be no point in submitting a budget that exceeded this standard.

God bless you and God bless a balanced buGod bless you . . . God bless you . . . . God bless the United States of America . . . God bless you . . . God bless you . . . God Bless you . . . God bless . . . God bless you . . . God bless you . . . God bless you . . . God bless the United States of America, the greatest nation in the world . . . God bless you . . . God Bless you / . . . God bless you . . . God bless you . . . and you . . . and you . . . God bless you . . . . God bless you . . . God bless you . . . God bless you . . . God bless, . . . God bless you . . . God bless you . . . God bless you . . . God bless. God bless you . . . God bless you, and you, and you . . . God bless you . . . blesyou . . . God bless you . . . God bless you . . . God bless you . . . G o d bless you . . . God bless you . . .

Question:

Mr. Mitchell—What is your position on abortion?

That's a very good question. From all the information that I have, the country is evenly divided on the question of abortion. From my understanding of the problem, half the people in our country want to have laws preventing abortions, and the other half believe that a woman has the right to choose. So what's the fair thing to do? I believe that, to satisfy both points of view, the only fair solution would be to permit abortions six months of the year, and abolish abortions the other six months. Let's say that a woman could have an abortion every other month and on alternate months she couldn't. This should satisfy both sides. God bless you.

God bless you . . . . God bless you . . . . God bless you . . . God bless you, my friend . . . . May God shine His countenance on you . . . God bless you . . . and you . . . . and you . . . . God bless all of you . . . . God bless you . . . God bless you . . . God bless you . . . God bless you . . . May God bless you always . . . Thank you, for your kind words . . . God bless you . . . God bless you . . . God bless you . . . thank you . . . thank you . . . God bless all of you . . . Yes, I do . . . God bless you . . . and you . . . and you . . . God bless you . . . . God bless you . . . God bless you, and your, and you . . . God bless all of you . . . Thanks for coming, and may God bless all of you. God bless you God bless you . . . God bless you . . . God bless you . . . God bless you . . . God bless you . . . That's a beautiful baby . . . God bless him . . . oh, it's a girl baby . . . God bless her . . . God bless you, and you, and you. (aside to aide) Can we move into a shady area? God bless you, and you.

Question: What's your position on capital punishment?

Mitchell: That's a very good question, and I don't know the answer. This is a country where everyone has a right to live in peace and security. When a person takes a life, he is depriving that person of his or her right to live in peace and security. A murderer should be punished. The bible says an eye for an eye and a tooth for a tooth. I don't know if that means capital punishment. I'll tell you this. There are murderers living on death row for years and years. It's costing the government millions of dollars to support these guys. How they get away with it, I don't know. What I would suggest is that we get together a severance package. Let's say we give the guy's estate, his wife and kids, a quarter of a million dollars. We could throw in some perks, like a fancy casket, and maybe two weeks of supervised play in Las Vegas. For this he lies down and takes the needle. It's no big deal. His family is well taken care of, he gets an all expense paid funeral, and we get to empty out death row. Everybody benefits. God bless you.

God bless you . . . God bless you . . . God bless all of you . . . No, I'm not related to that Mitchell . . . God bless you . . . God bless you . . . God bless you . . . God bless you, and you, and you . . . God bless every one of you . . . God bless . . . God bless . . . God bless you . . . God bless you . . . May God bless you with peace and prosperity . . . God bless you . . . and you and you . . . God bless you all . . . How do I know there's a God? I just know it . . . God bless you . . . God bless you, and you too . . . God bless you . . . Thank God for the United States of America . . . God bless you . . . . Thank God>>> God bless you, and you, and you . . . (aside to aide) Can we take a break? My hand is sore.>>> Thank you one and all . . . Thanks for coming. God bless you . . . God bless you

Question: Gay marriage. Are you for it, or against it?

Mitchell: That's a very good question. First, I always thought of marriage as a contract between a man and a woman. Having marriage between people of the same sex, I never thought about it. This may be something for God to deal with. God made man, and then He thought it would be a good idea for the man, Adam, to have a wife, Eve. Well, you know what happened, He took a rib from Adam and made a woman. If He thought that Adam needed another male for companionship, then He would have made another man. The point is that God made another human being with different plumbing than what he used to make Adam. If two people with the same plumbing want to get married, this is really a question for God. They should ask God for guidance. Is it OK for people who have the same plumbing to marry? He will tell them what to do. I believe in prayer. God bless you.

God bless you . . . God bless you . . . . God bless each and every one of you . . . God bless you . . . God bless you . . . My name is Alfred Mitchell and I'm running for president . . . God bless you God bless you . . . Oh, a beautiful baby, a girl . . . . I can tell because she's dressed in pink God bless you and your baby . . . God bless everyone here . . . God bless you, and thanks for coming, God bless you . . . Thanks for your good wishes, and may God bless you. Thank you, will try . . . God be with you, always . . . God bless you . . . God bless you . . . God bless you, and you anyou God bless you . . . God bless the good old U.S. of A . . . God Bless you > . . . May the good Lord bless you with good health, peace and prosperity . . . God bless you, and you, and you . . . God bless all of you . . . God bless you . . . Thanks for coming God bless you. God bless you

Question Mr. Mitchell, Do you believe that evolution should be taught in schools? Do you believe that Genesis should be taught in schools?

Mitchell—They are two very good questions. The key to the answer of both of these questions would be answered by posing a third question, and that is which came first, the chicken or the egg? In order to answer your questions, you would first have to determine the significance of the third question, namely the chicken/egg enigma. We can't expect our children to be exposed to Genesis or evolution instruction in the classroom without prior conditioning. This is particularly vital because we are a nation that consumes vast amounts of chickens and eggs. They are an important part of our diet, and pre-school children already know about chickens and eggs since these are established staples in practically every household in the country. There never has been a satisfactory answer to this question, yet people do eat chickens and eggs and just don't much concern themselves with which came first. God bless you.

God bless you, my friend. God bless you too. God bless you. God bless you. God bless you, and you, and you. God bless our great country. God bless the two of you. Hi there, God bless you. It sure looks like rain. I guess it would be welcome to our farmers. God bless you. God bless you. God bless you. Oh Martha's fine. I'll tell her you asked to be remembered. God bless you. God bless you. Don't forget to come out and vote. We can use all the help we can get. God bless you. God bless you. God bless you. God bless the United States of America. You say your name is Johnnie? God bless you, Johnnie. God bless you. God bless you. God bless the three of you.

Alfred did reply to questions, but always with the same bizarre answers. The media didn't know what to make of them, at first, but then the consensus seemed to be that this was Mitchell's way of avoiding committing himself on thorny questions. They thought he was being very clever to have conceived of this method of avoiding controversial issues that could prove damaging to his campaign. Was this a clever campaign tactic, or was Mitchell just being Mitchell?

And what was happening on the home front? Martha Mitchell had her routine, and, after getting used to the reality of having a husband who was the Democratic candidate for President of the United States of America, she settled into her regular routine, the highlight of which, was the bridge night with the ladies. Being a candidate's wife, she had to attend certain functions, express opinions, participate in photo ops, and generally make herself available as the campaign progressed. She did what was expected of her, and had someone at her side to guide her in her various activities.

Alfred occasionally came home for a breather. Shaking hands and bestowing the Lord's blessing, day after day, was a grueling routine, and he had to have breaks. The big problem was that his hand was very sore from all that hand shaking. It was especially painful shaking hands with an enthusiastic supporter with a very firm handshake. Then there were those who would take his hand and hold it while delivering words of wisdom. At home, he applied an ice bag to his hand to reduce the swelling, and relieve the soreness. He had vowed to shake every hand in America, and deliver a blessing, but it wasn't going to be easy.

Pollsters, at this stage of the race, had Anthony Brentwood leading Alfred Mitchell by six points. The Democratic Committee didn't think this was too bad, considering the inexperience of their candidate. In fact they thought he was doing much better than they had hoped. Alfred was working very hard, he had learned how to smile, and was able to relate to the voting public. Given the core support that they had from unions, plus issue oriented groups, they came to the conclusion that the continued invoking of God accounted for a better response from the public. Tacticians were at work trying to find additional ways of utilizing God in the campaign.

Martha had difficulty relating to her new situation. When Alfred left, surrounded by his bodyguards and advisors, it was as though he was a plumber responding to a frantic call from a customer whose hot water heater had sprung a leak and her basement was filling up with water. It was hard for her to conceive herself as occupying the White House as the First Lady.

Not so with Sarah Brentwood, the Republican candidate's wife. She had complete confidence that her husband would easily prevail, and that they would be white house residents for the next eight years. Sarah was a career lawyer, and was a managing partner in the prestigious law firm Chapel, Draper, Richter and Mellon. She was troubled by the demands of her career, and how she could balance her career with her responsibility of fulfilling the requirements of a first lady.

Susan and Meg, the two older children, were in college. At home were their twelve-year-old son, Brian Brentwood, and a very important member of the family, housekeeper Emma Raymond. Also, practically a member of the family was Tommy Osborne, Emma's trim, good looking special friend who she expected to marry when his divorce would be final. Tommy was a salesman for a manufacturer of designer aprons; Hyde Park, Ltd. His territory included New York and all of the New England States. He traveled when introducing a new line, to check store exposure or inventory levels, but had ample free time between trips. Consequently Tommy and Emma were able to spend much time together.

Sarah Brentwood was a very active member of her law firm, and was a lead attorney in arguments before the Supreme Court. She also was a gifted courtroom lawyer and was called on to represent some of the most difficult cases. She scrupulously avoided cases that would result in an adversarial involvement with the Attorney General, her husband. For this the Attorney General was most grateful.

Since there wasn't to be any debates, Tony Brentwood proposed three prime time talks, something like the Franklin D. Roosevelt fireside chats that were so effective. Tony suggested that the talks should be based on what he conceived to be the most pressing problems facing the nation today. It would take place in a living room atmosphere, without a flag draped in the background or any ostentatious ornamentation. He wanted it to be a person-to-person talk from his living room to the viewers' living room. The Republican party would make the arrangements for the time slots, and Tony would write the script for what he thought were the most important problems he would have to deal with, as an incoming president. The party leaders agreed that it could be very effective.

Tony Brentwood thought long and hard, deciding what one problem would be of such enormous importance that it would be the first order of business, on succeeding to the presidency. After considering problems, as he saw them, without question one had an urgency that dwarfed all others; the environment and global warming. In this respect he was at variance with his own party. In the Republican platform, passing reference was made to the environment. The Republicans thought it a global problem requiring consultation to determine if the environment was being affected, or whether it was a natural phenomenon of nature. Tony discussed this with party officials, and they finally agreed to allow Tony to work it out. The only stipulation they made was that they would want to see the script at least twenty-four hours before broadcast. Tony readily agreed

Tony divided his time between working on the three broadcasts and appearing at various functions with regard to advancing his run for the presidency. At home he worked hard to produce scripts that would reflect his views on what needed to be done, without regard for party philosophies. When he was in his study, and the door was closed, it was understood that he didn't want to be disturbed. Sometimes Tony would request a drink and something to nibble on, and Emma would take them to him. Otherwise the family would not disturb him,

Back at Grigsby, nothing much changed. The company was continuing to expand and was well regarded in the financial community. Dave Lambert could not assume the presidency, as it was still held by Alfred. Charles G. Cummins, a well-qualified young man, joined Grigsby Holdings in the post of Executive Vice President. David became interim president, pending the outcome of the election. They watched with intense interest a laughing, jovial Alfred, shaking hands, kissing babies, and invoking the Lord's blessing with each greeting. What to do if Alfred loses and elects to return to the company? It was impossible to know. This certainly was not the same Alfred who left to do his patriotic duty as a delegate to a party convention. With all of that, there was amazement and disbelief when they compared this Alfred with the Alfred they new. Bob Bento facetiously suggested that he could be assigned as Vice President in charge of kissing babies. At any rate, they all agreed that this was one of those situations where "you cross that bridge when you come to it."

Tony Brentwood decided that his first "fireside chat" would be the environment. In his mind, there was this huge ball in the sky, home to some six billion people, and the roof was badly in need of repair. This was the only home available and it had to be maintained. Tony did not want to talk in generalities. To simply say that there is an environmental problem would have little effect. They heard it before. What was needed was to pinpoint the problem, and offer a solution, a completely new way of dealing with environmental problems.

Automobiles and airplanes consumed vast amounts of gasoline, pumping heated fumes into the air, and causing the greenhouse affect. To limit the use of oil in such enormous amounts would require a change to a cleaner source of energy. Replacing oil with clean electricity could be the answer. How to make use of electricity and diminish the use of oil was a mammoth problem. Tony Brentwood thought about the world as it was before automobiles became so widespread.

Once the "horseless carriage" enjoyed huge acceptance, there was a corollary need for more, and better roads. This led to the development of the super highway, and, in turn, led to suburban sprawl. A man could enjoy rural living and, by use of the super highway, be in his office in twelve minutes. Early settlers did get to the office in twelve minutes, but not for long.

The super highways couldn't accommodate the huge number of cars entering the newly built highways. Traffic jams occurred daily. Tony thought about all of this. There was a need to develop a new way of transportation. It would have to offer advantages to interest motorists. Obviously a radical new way of travel, one that would be efficient, and drastically minimize our dependence on oil, would have to be proposed. What could that way of travel be? You can't tell people to stop using their cars. They know there's an environmental problem. They can't stop driving their cars. They have to be offered a new way to travel, yet be environmentally friendly. Tony thought of the changes that would have to be made. He knew that any ideas he proposed would be criticized, but if it made the environment talked about, and argued about, he would have achieved a significant milestone.

Chapter Eleven

The phone rings and Emma, the Brentwoods housekeeper, answers.

"Hello."

"Emma, Tom here, I have three tickets for tonight's ball game. I was going to take my kids. Larry can go, but Myra can't make it. She has other plans. That gives me one extra ticket. I thought Brian might like to join us."

"He can go if he finished his homework, and wants to go. Hold on and I'll check."

Emma returns.

"Tom, wild horses couldn't keep him away. He's already wearing a glove."

"I was lucky to get these tickets. They're box seats in back of third base, and this is an important game. Brian and Larry are about the same age, and I'm sure they'll get along fine."

"If Larry is anything like his father, I'm sure the kids will be great friends"

"Be right over."

The night was a little cool, just right for baseball. The seats were fabulous, in back of third base. The kids could reach over and make the attempt to glove a foul ball. On one attempt, about the fourth inning, the batter tried to bunt, and the ball rolled foul. As the ball rolled along the side, Larry had his glove down, and the ball took a little hop and nestled into the webbing of his glove. Larry had the first ball. The boys took turns examining the ball and thumping it into their gloves Shortly after, the ball girl fielded a foul, cleanly, and came over to the stands and put the ball in Brian's glove. Now, each of the boys had a big league baseball.

Going into the ninth inning, the teams were scoreless. Neither team could get a runner past second base. It was the end of the ninth and two were out. The home team had a man on second, but weren't able to advance him. Tom was concerned about the boys. If it went into extra innings the boys would be late getting home. They both had a big night. In addition to getting baseballs, the boys enjoyed hot dogs and soda pop. Tom lost count. With two out, the pitcher reared back and threw closer than he intended. The batter fell back to get out of the way, and the ball accidentally hit the fat of the bat. The ball arced over second base. The shortstop and second baseman ran frantically back, but the ball fell just beyond their reach. At the crack of the bat, the man on second took off like a shot, rounded third, and headed for home. The right fielder tried to get to the ball, hoping to make a play at the plate. Before he reached the ball, he saw the runner about to cross home plate. He had no play, so he didn't even bother to pick up the ball. The game was over. The home team won.

Tom was relieved. The game didn't go into extra innings. They could all go home. Tom hoped that there wouldn't be any after effects from what the boys had been munching on during the game.

There wasn't.

Emma had known Tom only a little over two months. Tom moved into the area. Being a gregarious person (a salesman), Tom had to be with people, so he joined the church that Emma attended. He was there every Sunday. When they sang hymns, Tom's rich baritone voice could be heard above the others. He also attended the Tuesday Social. After a brief service, they all went into the recreation hall to dine on the lavish array of food, prepared by the women. The food was served buffet style. After filling their plates, they would take a seat at a table. Tom circulated a lot, but often found a seat with Emma.

After dining, Tom would go into the kitchen, roll up his sleeves, and go to work. Emma had always gone into the kitchen for clean up. Tom was a welcome newcomer. In addition to helping in the kitchen, he folded and stacked chairs, and used the push broom to clean the floor area. He had a talent for getting things done, and they found that clean up time was somewhat less. Tom and Emma soon found that they had an affinity for each other. Emma welcomed the attention, and they soon became a caring, devoted couple. Nothing was said about marriage. Tom was involved with his divorce. Emma expected to marry Tom, once the divorce was final.

Tom was accepted as one of the family, picking up Emma for a night out, or just doing some errand for Emma. The Brentwoods got to know Tom, and they thought both Emma and Tom were just right for each other.

On one occasion, Tom brought a stack of designer aprons into the church, a contribution that was made by Tom's company. They were sold to the Congregationalists for six dollars each, half the regular price of twelve dollars. The proceeds were given to the church. The aprons very quickly sold out. On another occasion Emma happened to mention to Tom that there was a need for some shelving in the garage to get things off the floor. The next day Tom came to the house with some lumber. Within a few hours, Tom completed the shelving, and the items were off the floor. Although Emma was pleased with the results, she was unhappy that Tom had responded to an off hand remark.

"I'll have to watch myself. I didn't mean for you to do it," she said.

Chapter Twelve

The day of the first of the three talks arrived. Tony had given the Republican officials the script for his first person to person talks. The officials were quite concerned about the subject matter. They met with Tony to talk about the script.

"You are making the environment your number one priority above all other issues. We're still trying to determine the extent to which global warming is a problem. What you're proposing is a radical departure from the way oil is used today. From a political standpoint, your proposal may disturb the voter to the extent that he could be turned off by so radical a proposal. We're doing well. The surveys indicate that we have a comfortable lead. Why rock the boat?" said George Pommeroy, chairman of the Republican Party.

"I can't be concerned about the politics of this campaign. From everything that I have read, global warming is a real problem, and it is causing many unwanted changes. If my proposals cost us votes, that is a small price to pay. We have to change. We must put a stop to our dependence on oil. There is no easy answer," said Tony.

"The hybrid car and windmills are one answer. Ethanol is another. These are changes that the public could accept. What you're suggesting is a radical change. Do you think the public is ready for it? Do you think they'll understand what you're proposing? Frankly, I had trouble understanding it myself. It may be a worthwhile project for the future, but if the problem is as urgent as you believe, then we ought to stay with what we know, and what is doable." said Senator Max Hellman.

Tony threw his hands up. "Nothing that I'm suggesting is chiseled in stone. Everything is on the table. I'm suggesting a concept that could end our dependence on oil. The hybrid car is an advance, but sales are limited, as they seem to be. Ethanol and windmills are real possibilities, but there is no sense of urgency, no feeling that they must be developed to the fullest. Windmills are a proven source of energy, but there's "not in my backyard" opposition. Atomic energy plants have proven value, but again there's "not in my backyard" resistance. I thought about emphasizing these in my talk, but I didn't think they would work. They heard it all before. That's why I'm suggesting a new concept, a radical new approach. You don't understand it, Max, I have trouble understanding it myself. The point is that I want to get people fired up. I want them talking about this new concept and whatever else they think will work. Above all, I want them to feel this sense of urgency. We have to get off dead center. What I'm suggesting is a radically new approach to the problem. I'm not looking for adherents to my proposal. I do want people to be up in arms and talking, talking about the environment and recognizing that it is a problem of great urgency.

"You can't ignore the political problems a backlash could cause. You're running for president, but a lot of congressmen and senators have their career s on the line. They're running for office too. We're comfortably ahead. It just doesn't make sense to gamble with our future," said the Senator.

"Global warming is a real problem, and it's been ignored for too long. I don't claim to have the definitive solution. I do have a concept that has possibilities, and that's the way I expect to present it. If a better way surfaces, I'm listening. I just want our dependence on oil to come to a screeching halt. And I want our people to change the way they go to and from their work. I can't be concerned about how my broadcast will be accepted. The problem is real, and something has got to be done about it," said Tony.

They argued for about an hour. Tony couldn't be budged. In the end they grudgingly gave in. They just hoped that Tony would do a convincing job, avoiding a backlash.

The day of the broadcast arrived. Tony would broadcast from the Brentwood living room. There was no flag in the background. In back of the soft chairs was a reproduction of Seurat's "Sunday in the park." The setting was informal. Tony wanted the focus to be on him, and what he had to say, and didn't want any distractions.

The broadcast people moved in with long lengths of cables, cameras, and electronic equipment. A truck, with transmission gear was parked in the driveway. With everything in readiness Tony began his broadcast.

He started by talking about the environment; global warming evidence that was proven by reliable sources. It was no longer a question of whether global warming was taking place. The evidence was overwhelming. The problem was oil." We no longer have the luxury of being completely dependent on oil. We must develop a new, super clean source of power." He went on to say that this was one area that needs to be explored. "We have to make bold decisions and make a clean break with the past." He then described typical traffic patterns that were resulting in pumping hot contaminate into the atmosphere. He cited the tie-ups in driving during rush hours when cars travel almost bumper-to-bumper, very often in first gear for long periods of time. Problems arise as a result of accidents, police activity or mainly just too many cars occupying a limited space. Most cars have just one passenger, the driver.

What Tony suggested was a completely new way of transporting people from origination to destination. There would be three categories that would have to be developed. First would be the design of a car. Second would be the network to transport thousands of vehicles in use at any given time. Third would be the enormous amount of electricity needed to service the system. Also needed would be the establishment of an Authority to arrange financing, supervise research and management.

The vehicles Tony talked about were radically different from the cars we're familiar with today. Most of the cars would be small, of a size to accommodate one passenger. The vehicles would be the property of the Authority and, for an annual fee, those who choose to be a part of the system would have unlimited use. The cars would b cleaned and maintained by the Authority. The user would have no obligation whatsoever, insurance, inspections, repairs or the periodic fill at the gas station, just to name a few. The cars would be battery operated for secondary driving.

"What I'm suggesting," said Tony, "is a completely new way of commuting, a system that would be more efficient for you. It would work something like this. You leave your house in the morning, as you usually do, and get into a car provided for you. You then drive this battery-operated car to the nearest terminal. At the terminal you would be served a pre-ordered breakfast tray and a newspaper. At this point you would push an appropriate button to indicate the terminal you want to exit. You are then entered into the system. You do no driving. At this point your car is programmed to take you to the terminal you indicated. You relax, eat your breakfast, and read your newspaper. On arrival, you leave for secondary driving to your destination. The car is picked up, taken to the terminal, cleaned and the battery is on the charger. At the end of day, a car is left for you, to drive to the terminal, and enters the system for the return trip home. All of this is done without the deadly emissions from tail pipes. There are no tail pipes. There are no engines powered by gasoline. Transportation is achieved by an external source of power, electricity.

"So, to make all of this possible, we have to have an adequate source of electricity. The two main sources of energy that are talked about today are windmill farms, and nuclear energy. Windmill farms are in use today, in some parts of the world, and are producing needed energy. Nuclear plants are operating successfully throughout the world. The problem is that, here at home, no new nuclear plants are being built. Even if a new plant would be started, it would be years before it would be put into service. After what happened in Russia, there is much fear and opposition to nuclear power plants being built. I think that in all these years we have demonstrated that nuclear plants can be operated safely. Nuclear plants, today, are an important source of power. Our need for clean power is urgent and we have to make use of what is available. Right now the most promising are windmill farms. Other sources of energy are solar and ethanol. Scientists, I'm sure, will make valuable contributions in developing clean energy sources.

The most difficult part of this program would be devising a system that would transport cars, electronically and efficiently. For this we would have technical people develop a system that would do the job. There have been some developments. The Japanese have developed a system that uses magnetic levitation to propel trains without contact with the tracks. I don't know how successful this method is, but it is an innovation. Of course, another possibility could be some overhead suspension system, something like the cable cars that go from peak to peak. How to devise a system would have to be the work of technical people.

Making all of this possible could be a government project, with a sizeable budget to fund the cost of the project, or it could be an Authority to float bonds and have it privately funded. Here we would have to have financial people involved in advising us how to fund the project. If a system like this is adopted, there would be revenue developed through user fees.

I want to thank you for listening to me. What I have suggested could be considered revolutionary, a plan that is not doable. That may be so. I don't know what plan could evolve that would eliminate our total dependence on the automobile. My concern was to find a way to stop this disastrous dependence on oil. The environment, global warming, are crucial problems, we cannot afford a policy of live today and let tomorrow take care of itself. We owe it to our children to do what we can to give them a house without the problems that we are trying to deal with, today. I don't care what plan is put into effect. If it will deal with the problem more efficiently than what I have proposed, then it will have my complete support. Thanks for hearing me out, and the next administration, Republican or Democratic, will have to find a solution to global warming. We must not let it continue. Good night and God bless this world, with its six billion brothers and sisters."

The Democrats were allotted ten minutes for rebuttal. Senator Harry B. Grady was the Democratic choice to comment on the speech immediately after it was concluded. The Senator agreed that the environment, with global warning and the greenhouse effect, were causing very serious problems.

The Senator said "I want to compliment Anthony Brentwood on his excellent presentation. We, in the Democratic Party, have long expressed our concern about environmental problems. We were gratified to hear him express his views, which, incidentally, are not those of the Republican Party. They do not express the same sense of urgency that Anthony Brentwood and we both feel.

Now as to what Mr. Brentwood proposed. We are to have a new type of car, not yet invented. Thousands of these vehicles are to enter a system, not yet invented. These cars will be transported by some method, not yet invented. Huge amounts of electricity will be needed to supply power to this massive, spider-web array of lines, to come from some source, not yet established, This is an excellent concept, proposed by a man who is both dedicated and imaginative, but even if we started tonight, and shoveled the first spade-full of dirt, to dig the first foundation of who knows what, at the very earliest we possibly could have something going, on a very limited scale, would be, at the very least, fifteen years before this system could be made operable. We can't wait fifteen years. We can't wait ten years. The urgency is such that we can't wait five years. We have to go with what we know now. Do the words ethanol, hydrogen, hybrid cars sound familiar to you? What if we put the automobile manufacturers to work to build nothing but hybrid cars? What if we make it mandatory that gas powered cars be taken off the road within a specified time period? We already know that windmill farms can be an effective way to harness prevailing winds to produce sizeable amounts of energy. This will work. This will harness energy. This is currently being used successfully in other parts of the world. So what are we waiting for? If we're serious about reducing our dependence on oil, lets get the gas-guzzlers off the road. Let's make auto racing illegal. Let's do what we know we can do, now. With Anthony Brentwood's speech tonight, we can assume that the Republicans are now ready to join ranks with the Democrats, to do what needs to be done to repair the house all of us live in.

Again, I want to congratulate Anthony Brentwood for taking a giant step toward waking up our country as to the very real problems with global warming. He did the world a great service in alerting us to the need to act, now. It was refreshing to hear a revolutionary solution to the problem. I don't agree with it. Too much time would be taken up in the massive details that would have to be worked up. We don't know what to expect, what problems could arise. The environment is no longer an issue between Republicans and Democrats. Let's unite, and do what we know how to do, and let's do it now. Are you ready, Anthony Brentwood? Are you ready, Republican Party? We, the Democratic Party, we are ready. We are thankful for this opportunity to comment on Anthony Brentwood's talk, and to offer some suggestions of our own. Whatever you think about what you heard tonight, Tony Brentwood deserves a lot of credit for finally clearing the air on global warming. It is an urgent problem and it has to be aggressively addressed. This he did for us. God bless the United States of America, and God bless all of you who listened to what we had to say. And God bless Anthony Brentwood for his courageous disregard for political considerations and making global warming his first priority. Good night."

News item

Republican candidate Anthony Brentwood took to the airways, last night, to alert the world that the house all of us live in, is badly in need of repairs. He did exactly that. Not only was emphasis placed on the very real problem of global warming, and the greenhouse effect, but also he offered a concept of his own. If what he suggested could be achieved, our dependence on foreign oil would come to a screeching halt. Comments were mixed. There were serious question whether America would willingly give up its love affair with the automobile. This would be a radical departure from the way America lives. Even though the benefits could be substantial, would this new system of daily commuting work for the traveler? What Brentwood suggested was a completely different way of traveling. In this concept, ownership of a car would be the property of a central Authority. The subscriber would have use of it for an annual fee. The advantages of this system are, no maintenance costs, no cars to wash and vacuum, no periodic visits to a gas station, no driving (the car is electronically programmed), and, of course, does not use oil derivatives. This system would be powered by electricity from nuclear plants, and/or windmill farms.

The disadvantage, as Senator Grady pointed out, this is a concept, and a vast amount of research would have to be done in order to make the system operable. Senator Grady estimated that it would take at least fifteen years before a working model could be produced. The problem of global warming is an urgent problem and has to be resolved by what is immediately available.

Professor Michael Chambers, Dean of the school of Engineering, Burwell University, said he did watch Anthony Brentwood's program. The central theme of his talk was the very serious environmental problems that have to be corrected. His remedy was very interesting, but I'm inclined to agree with the senator that completion would be years away. We can't afford to wait. There are too many problems to be worked out. We would need a large staff, to begin with, just to identify the problems. For instance, a project such as this would involve the acquisition of huge amounts of real estate, much of it in populated areas. This would be needed just to construct conveniently located terminals, readily accessible for secondary driving. The end result, however, if it could be achieved, would be a greatly improved transportation system. Putting an astronaut on the moon was a lot less complicated. Tony Brentwood was to be commended for conveying an urgent need to get moving on the problem of global warming. It was a wake-up call.

News Item

OPEC Calls

Emergency Meeting

Paris—AS a result of last night's talk by Tony Brentwood, the oil producing nations were very much concerned about the future of oil. If the Republican candidate's campaign would be successful, and Tony Brentwood became the next president, or even if the Democrats should succeed to the presidency, they could adopt a program that would drastically reduce the consumption of oil. Because of the uncertainty OPEC decided to call an emergency meeting to see what they need to do to counteract this threat to their oil business. Clearly, it would not be in their interest to see an alternative to the use of oil adopted.

* * *

News Item

Brentwood Campaign

Sees Surge In Polling

Pollsters sampling of response to Tony Brentwood's speech found the response to the upside. The new poll shows Tony Brentwood leading rival, Alfred Mitchell, by ten points. The new result is fifty-five to forty-five. Most people interviewed accepted the urgency to make the needed changes. There was general acceptance that there is global warming and there is a great need to free ourselves of our dependence on oil. They weren't sure that Tony Brentwood's concept is the way to go, but there was a feeling that it would serve as a starting point, and that it had to be done.

News item

Peter D. Block, Executive Director of the Used Car Dealer's Friendship Society, said that their members were being swamped with calls from motorists wanting to sell their cars. Many television viewers believed that the Brentwood plan was being adopted. They feared that the price of cars would drop drastically. They wanted to sell while the market for used cars held up. Conversely buyers of used cars were not visiting used car lots. Dealers were reporting a sharp reduction in sales. Block estimated that this unusual situation would correct in a week or two.

* * *

RANDOM COMMENTS FROM INTERVIEWS

Philadelphia Inquirer—Charlie Lemon, (gas station operator) "Yeh, I heard Tony Brentwood[s speech. I aint no spring chicken, but I don't think I'll see the day that I'll have to close up my station because there aint anybody out there pumping gas."

Boston Globe—Michael Ferry. Harvard Senior, "We get a lot of snow around here. How the hell are you going to do any secondary driving with a foot of snow on the ground and you're battling the elements in a glorified golf cart."

Baltimore Sun—Tina Suttley—School Teacher—Nothing will change here. Our kids get bussed to school. They wouldn't fit into any transportation system. What we're doing now would continue.

Philadelphia Daily News—Bill Kramer—Taxi Driver—What goes around, comes around. Even though it may take years to build I think they should get started now. My only concern is with the companies that would get contracts. In the past, problems with quality always surfaced. I hope that quality control experts will make sure that we get what we're paying for.

USA Today—Carl Bentley—Purchasing Agent "He lost me. Somewhere in his talk, I fell asleep."

Chicago Tribune—Connie Linton, Nurse, "He said that global warming was real and it has to be stopped. I agree with him 100 percent."

Seattle Times—Al Gonzolas—Plumber—"I don't know. I was watching a ball game. What did he say?"

Sacremento Bee—Marvin Grossman—Commercial Artist—I was impressed with his sincerity. He really cares. He has my vote."

Los Angeles Times—Liz Blavis—Personnel Manager—He really focused on the problem and gave us some very convincing ideas about what could be done. I would willingly enlist into his program, however it comes out. He's a winner in my book.

Miami Herald—Leon Porter—Engineer—He outlined the basis of a well conceived program that is doable. He has outlined three main segments, the vehicle, the operational system, and the power source. Above all is the establishment of an authority to provide the funds to make all of this possible. This is the first real attempt to do something about global warming. I welcome it.

St. Petersburg Times—Arthur Jefferson—Store manager—He's gonna stack those cars one on top of another? This I gotta see, if I live that long.

St. Louis Post Dispatch—Phil Bowman—Barber—Personally, I wouldn't be affected. Our living quarters are upstairs, and travel to work is minimal. But, broadly, one couldn't miss how effective he was in giving us the problem and a possible solution. The sincerity of the man was obvious. I'm with him.

New York Times—Ted Reynolds—Chairman of the Democratic Committee.—Sure I heard his talk; every bit of it, from beginning to end. I have great doubts about the sincerity of those in his party, with whom he will have to work and have their full support. Actually, what he was proposing is the Democratic position. All you have to do is refer to the platforms of both parties. The Republican Party hardly mentions the environment, and as far as global warming is concerned there is no indication that they really see it as a problem. The Democratic platform looks at the problem differently. We are very much concerned about the environment, and want our many waters restored so that fish can live in them and people can utilize them for bathing and limited recreation. As far as global warming is concerned, our platform specifically states that it is very real, and that an intense effort must be made to do whatever it takes to make the necessary changes.

What the Republican candidate is doing is running as a Democrat. He has taken our program and is proposing it as his own. If he should be elected, he would have to deal with the oil barons who pretty much control Congress. The lobbyists are doing a good job. No way would he be able to prevail over big oil. Read the planks of both parties. We're for doing what has to be done about global warming. They are not.

Letters To The Editor

Dear Sir:

I know you won't print this letter, but I'm going to write it anyway. I don't know what the hell you guys are doing, making a big deal about global warming. You know damn well that there is nothing wrong with the environment. Nobody ever proved that there is global warming. All you're doing is scaring the hell out of people. You go back in history. Go way back. We always had changes in the weather, so what's the big deal?

About this gas business, I drive one of those cars you guys call gas guzzlers. I work my butt off, all week, in a steel mill. Comes the weekend I want to relax, so I get in my car and drive, on the road or off the road, it makes no difference, and I don't worry about gas. There are plenty of gas stations out there that welcome my business.

And they're going to get it, for years to come.

Bud Pritchard

* * *

News item

Paris—The much heralded emergency meeting of the OPEC nations ended without any decisions being made. One proposal suggested reducing production levels to the extent where the price of a barrel of this very scarce oil would reach one hundred dollars a barrel. By making oil very expensive, they reasoned, gasoline could only be afforded by people of means, thereby limiting car usage. OPEC would be making its contribution to limiting global warming. Objections to this proposal centered on the certainty that this would cause a worldwide depression and would be counter—productive. In effect, it would be "killing the goose that laid the golden egg."

Another proposal was to increase production to the extent that oil would be very cheap, the reasoning there would be, that with low gasoline prices, users would be less concerned about global warming. This proposal found few supporters. They didn't want to upset the environmentalists.

Finally, they agreed that there was nothing that needed agreement. They decided that the public's love affair with the automobile was so strong that no proposed change would affect the situation, no matter what suggestions are adopted. They hastily adjourned so that middle east member s could get back home in time for the camel races.

* * *

New Item

New York—Martha Mitchell bought ten boxes of Girl Scout cookies. When the door-bell rang, a smiling "lady of the house" greeted a group of girls with cookies to sell. "I'll take ten boxes." She paid the girls and said, "My husband loves cookies. I'm sure he'll enjoy eating them." The girls left, and the door was closed.

* * *

News Item

New York—Grigsby Holdings announced that its Grigsby Construction division has received clearances for the proposed construction of an office complex in Orlando, Florida. Spokesman for the company said they would be breaking ground in one week.0

* * *

News item

The proposed windmill farm, to be established five miles off the coast of Newport, Rhode Island, was strongly opposed by the residents. They did not want their view of the ocean cluttered with a lot of windmills. They said they were sympathetic to the need for windmills and would probably find them acceptable if they were at least fifty miles off the coast.

News item

Question Mr. Mitchell, a spokesman for the Necktie Manufacturers Guild was very critical of captains of industry appearing on television in a casual shirt, and without a tie. Sales of ties have plummeted. Factories are down to seventeen percent of capacity. Manufacturers are desperate. Workers are demanding action from their union. They don't give ties for Christmas anymore. As president, what would you do about it?

Mitchell That's a very good question. As you can see, I am wearing a tie. I did receive a call from someone from the Necktie Manufacturers Guild. They made a study and found that sixty-two percent of high school graduates did not know how to tie a tie. This was an alarming development. He suggested that it be made part of the curricula, that no boy should be permitted to graduate without demonstrating that he knew how to properly tie a tie.

You never can tell when a tie can come in handy. I remember, one time, I was driving along and my muffler and tail pipe came loose and were clanging on the road. I pulled over to the side, took off my tie, and tied the tail pipe to the chassis. As president I would urge important people to be properly dressed with a tie. You never can predict when a tail pipe and muffler would come loose and you would need a tie to anchor it to the chassis. Of course you could say, you could use a belt, but it's not the same. A belt is essential to keeping your pants from dropping.

God bless you . . . God bless you . . . God bless you . . . and you . . . God bless you . . . God bless you . . . God bless the United States of America . . . God bless you . . . May God shine his countenance upon you . . . You're a beautiful family . . . God bless you all . . . God bless you . . . God bless you . . . God bless you, and you, and you. God bless you . . . Thanks for coming out . . . God bless you . . . Be the good Lord willing, we will win in November . . . God bless you . . . God bless you, and thanks for your support . . . God bless you all . . . God bless you, and you.

News Item

—Work at the Peerless Paper Products Co. logging camp was halted because it was discovered that the rare flacker bird was nesting atop some of the trees being harvested. Bird watchers made the discovery and notified the company. Work will resume only after the company is given clearance by the "Save Our Flackers" Society. Both candidates were made aware of the problem. Neither offered any comment. Mitchell did say he enjoyed hearing birds chirping.

* * *

News Item

Candidate Mitchell
Kisses 1000th Baby

El Paso, Texas—This was a significant day, achieved by Alfred Mitchell in his race for the presidency. He kissed his 1000th baby. Mitchell was unaware that a milestone had been reached. The announcement was made by Dom Pinelli, spokesman for the Bottomly Co., manufacturer of the "User-Friendly" brand diapers. The company recorded every occasion when Mitchell had kissed a baby, and Dom Pinelli was there for this memorable event, the kissing of the 1000th baby.

When Irma Fliegel placed her three month old baby, Lucy Fliegel, into Alfred's arms, she had no idea that it was a significant occasion. She was there because she heard that it was "good luck" for a baby to be kissed by a presidential candidate.

Dom Pinelli made the announcement to the cheering crowd, and announced that Mrs. Fliegal would receive a year's supply of the "User Friendly" Diapers. Irma Fliegel was overjoyed at her good fortune, and kissed both Dom Pinelli, and Alfred Mitchell. "Baby" Lucy Fliegal slept through the entire event.

Chapter Thirteen

The first broadcast Tony made had all of the elements of a crisis. We were at the eleventh hour, and there was a problem that demanded immediate action. Something had to be done to stem the relentless effect of global warming. We were seeing the melting of frozen areas that were in a solid, frozen state for eons. Tony Brentwood's second broadcast would be important, but in no way have the urgency of the same magnitude. In fact, there were issues that needed to be addressed, but it was a toss-up as to which one Tony would choose. Certainly healthcare would be high on the list. Also, to a lesser degree, would be immigration problems, the unbalanced budget, and the mounting deficit in our balance of trade. Tony made his decision. It would be the UN.

For this talk the house was set up very much as the first one. Cables were strung, leading to the truck parked in the driveway. Lighting, cameras, and electronic equipment were positioned for the broadcast. At the appointed time, Tony was introduced, and the camera focused on him. On cue, he started his talk.

"Friends, tonight I want to talk about a subject that has been troubling me for some time. Although the United Nations has done many good things since it was established, there are areas where, by the nature of its basic structure, it was unable to deal with problems that reflected the reason why it was established in the first place. To keep the peace, to deal with famine, to be concerned about the basic needs of an oppressed people, these were areas where dictators claimed immunity because the activities were "internal affairs." In these cases the UN is powerless to act.

It is extremely difficult to reason with representatives of countries that maintain a tight, ironclad grip on their people, and conduct affairs based on their selfish interests. It is my belief that no nation should have membership in a world body, such as the United Nations, that doesn't have completely free elections, free of coercion, free of control of the media, no threat of political imprisonment, and certainly no tampering with the ballot boxes. Because of this unacceptable situation, I believe that we should withdraw our membership in the United Nations.

I would, with consultation with countries that do have free elections, suggest the formation of a new world body, the United Democratic Nations. Membership in this body would be open to all countries that are completely free, and where those in power accept the decisions made by the electorate. We would meet with the present UN on matters where there was a common interest, and where our involvement could be helpful. It just doesn't make sense for free nations to adjust to the level where deliberations are hampered by countries in the steel grip of ruthless dictators."

Tony went on to cite instances where there was a need for a common understanding of problems that needed to be considered, but were tabled because of opposition from dictatorially oriented countries. Also, there is the matter of corruption in high places. Our country has made attempts to have this mess cleaned up, but we were unsuccessful.

Although there has been widespread dissatisfaction with the United Nation's inability to function in accordance with democratic standards, its existence had been accepted as a compromise.

Some good results have been achieved, but there have been glaring failures. Tony Brentwood was convinced we could do better.

The Republican candidate brought up a subject that had been troubling him.

Also, I think there is another related area that needs to be considered, and that is the positioning and active use of our military, down through the years. The big question is "are we the policeman of the world?" During the Truman administration the answer was "yes." We were involved with the war in Korea. There were other police actions that were taken. We stepped in to replace England when Greece needed help. And then. of course, there was our tragic experience in Viet Nam. The French had been soundly defeated, and we, as "policeman of the world" took over and our failure was even more disastrous than the French experience. More recently, our involvement in Iraq is a tragic experience. In each of these incursions, we experienced a great loss of life, young men and women whose lives were sacrificed in causes that were questionable. Their loss is a wake-up warning. We may not be the policemen of the world.

Our military is stationed all over the world. We are supporting governments with our military and our dollars. As president, I will carefully evaluate the entire situation. Are our military needed? Do we need to export our dollars? Above all, are we protecting countries that can well afford to pay for the protection they are getting? These are problems that have to be carefully evaluated. I will accept nothing on the basis of "that's always the way it was done. I value the life of every man, woman, and child. No one will have to put his life on the line for a questionable objective. Not on my watch. We are propping up countries with outlays of millions of dollars. Identifying those countries, and determining the justification for our continued support, will get early consideration in my administration Thank you and good-night. 1

At the conclusion of the broadcast, the Democratic spokesman was in a position where he could agree with Tony or defend the United Nations. The spokesman, Senator Charles Strickland, was in a situation where he wouldn't do either.

"Much of what you heard tonight is true. The United Nations is not, by any means, a democratic body. There are small, democratic countries that are discriminated against by a powerful group of dictatorships that influence the direction of the United Nations. There's no argument about that. What Tony Brentwood did say was the widespread corruption that is damaging the very framework of this body. Even when uncovered, and admitted that corruption exists, the leadership is helpless to do anything about it. No question. The United Nations is very badly in need of an overhaul.

So what do we do about it? Tony Brentwood advocates the withdrawal of nations that would meet the criteria of being truly democratic, and the formation of a new United Nations, The United Democratic Nations. By doing this, he is leaving a body that would be completely in control of dictatorship countries that constitute more than half the world's population. Can we desert them? I don't think so. When you think of the rampant corruption, you can only stand by and hold your nose. Tony Brentwood's reasoning has merit. Perhaps a change is timely. Given the responsibility of doing what we can to help people to a better life, it probably would be better, more effective, to work from within the organization.

Tony Brentwood brought up another question that deserves a thorough revue. We are not the policemen of the world. We are the conscience of the world. In this respect, Tony Brentwood deserves credit for bringing it to the attention of all of us. We can't ask any of our military to put their lives on the line for causes that should be the concern of the United Nations. That's where it belongs. That's where we, as a great power, a great power with a conscience, can use our influence on matters that are of concern to all of us, people everywhere. I thank Tony Brentwood for, once again, giving us much to think about. And I thank the Republican Party for the opportunity afforded us to comment on their candidate's broadcast. Goodnight to all of you.

The pollsters again recorded favorable reaction to the speech. After the talk on the environment, the reading was fifty-five to forty-five percent. In recent days it had narrowed somewhat. Alfred's God and Country campaigning was having some positive results, keeping him in contention. In addition, strong campaigning by the Democratic rank and file was effective. After the talk on global warming, the Democrats attacked the oil companies, accusing them of lobbying and influencing Congress. They were responsible for environmental problems. By pointing a finger at big oil, they had gained back some of the points they had lost. Now with Tony Brentwood's reasoned speech on the UN, and our policy of 'policemen f the world, pollsters reported the Republicans back to fifty-five to forty-five, a comfortable margin. Aside from the content of the talks, what made them so effective was that Tony looked directly into the camera, and the viewer had the feeling that Tony was talking to him, and to him alone. With Election Day fast approaching, there didn't seem any possibility for the Democratic candidate to overcome the ten-point spread. Tony Brentwood's strategy was working.

Chapter Fourteen

With the campaign progressing so favorably, the Brentwood's had a bright future. Tony was hard at work, making plans for the new administration, so that he could, as the old cliché had it, "hit the ground running." The third, and last talk to the American people covered a variety of issues that Tony intended to deal with. There were no blockbusters, as in the first two talks. The pollsters were unanimous in predicting a Republican victory, although none were talking landslide, remembering the Tom Dewey fiasco.

In the back of the house, Brian and Tom were having a catch with the new ball Brian acquired at the stadium. Emma was greatly concerned about Tom as he seemed to be depressed. Looking out the window, she could tell that his movements were that of a man whose energy level was low. Sure enough, Tom ended the session, claiming that he had to go somewhere, some appointment. He apologized to Brian and left. He didn't come into the house to tell Emma that he was leaving. She had noticed this very worried look, completely foreign to the Tom she knew. He was always so cheerful, so dynamic in his interaction with people. This change was sudden, totally unexpected.

Emma thought that perhaps there was some problem with the divorce. She knew that she wasn't the cause of his depression. He had assured her of that, and she knew him well enough to know that he loved her. She didn't know what was wrong. He wouldn't talk about it. He had the look of a man who was told, by his doctor, that his illness was terminal. Tom had assured Emma that his problem had nothing to do with health, or his position with his company.

When Tom ended his play with Brian, he walked off, and that was the last Emma would see of Tom Osborne. He walked off and kept walking. He just walked, aimlessly, down one street and up another, being jostled by the crowded sidewalk, not knowing where he was going, just completely involved with a very serious problem that had no solution. He found a bench and sat down. He was badly shaken. His situation was hopeless.

The name he had used, during the past few months, Tom Osborne, was not his real name. His real name was Thomas R. Jamison. He was not a salesman for an apron manufacturer. The apron manufacturer did not exist. It was a fictitious company suggested by his editor. The editor also provided the aprons Tom donated to his congregation. The editor also gave Tom the baseball tickets. Tom was not in the midst of a divorce. He was a happily married man. His real occupation was investigative reporter, and his employer, at that time, was TELL Publications. His assignment was to integrate himself into the Brentwood household.

A few days ago, he had a meeting with his editor. The editor was ecstatic. He showed Tom photographs, and Tom was shocked.

"You can't use these photographs. You just can't," said Tom.

"The hell we can't," said the editor with a big grin.

Tom had thought that the worst possible photograph would be, perhaps; Tony cleaning his nose. That would have been the end of it. These photographs were totally unexpected. He hadn't an inkling of what was going on behind the closed door of Tony Brentwood's study. Tom was both shocked and angry. They probably had some idea about this, that's why they went to such great lengths to get photographs. The editor would not tell Tom how the photographs were obtained. Also Tom had not been previously informed of their suspicions as to what was going on behind the closed door.

"How we got the photographs is none of your business," said the editor bluntly

"You can't do this to the Brentwood's. They're a wonderful family. This will ruin them."

The editor was unmoved. "As an investigative reporter, you're not permitted the luxury of falling in love with your targets. You should know that. We have an issue to put out. This one will be explosive, a real blockbuster."

He thought of the hurt that it would cause Emma and the Brentwood family. It was painful and heart breaking. Yes, he had fallen in love with his targets. It wasn't difficult. They were a loveable family.

"If you release these photographs, there very well could be a backlash. You could be held responsible for invading private property. There could even be a congressional investigation. No question, The Republicans would see to it that there would be a congressional investigation, and this could very well ruin TELL publication. It's not worth the risk to publish these photographs," Tom argued.

"That's not my business. My job is to get the evidence, get the facts, even shade them when necessary, but get it in shape so it can hit the street. That's what's happening here. The guys upstairs are on top of this, and I have a green light. Five days before election, we're coming out with a special edition, and every super-market will be loaded with copies. I don't give a damn about the election; the backfiring, congressional inquiries or anything else. I do my job, and you did yours." And then, with a twinkle in his eye, the editor added, "And I'll see to it that you get full credit for this exposure. You did a first rate job, and we're very proud of you."

Tom left the TELL offices totally defeated. He knew that they would run the special edition five days before the election. Tony would be in a state of shock; as would the Brentwood family. There would not be sufficient time to re-group, to try to hold on enough to win the election. Tom thought about leaking the coming expose to the press. This would play into the hands of TELL publications. They would deny having any knowledge of photographs and issue "teaser" releases up to the date of publication. There was nothing he could do to escape from this coming tragedy. He, himself; would be publicized as the very clever reporter who was able to uncover this incredible story.

Tom was devastated. These were very clever people, and they would do what Tom was told they would do. Tom knew that when the special issue became available, the wide margin that Tony enjoyed, would very quickly evaporate. There would be frantic conferences on how to counteract this bad publicity, and salvage enough votes to squeeze through. Tom could not conceive an effective explanation for this.

TELL Publications had visual evidence, and they had the experience to know how to use it effectively. This was an extremely difficult situation, and it would take people skilled in the art of damage control to deal with the problem.

Tom wondered if, in some way, it would be helpful to tell Tony about the photographs and the coming special edition. At least, he would be forewarned and would have time to prepare for it. By doing this, Tom would be revealing his true identity, and his reason for intruding the Brentwood household. What he did was reprehensible and unforgivable. They were going to know the truth about him, so it would be better that they got it from him, rather than from TELL.

Tom went to the Brentwood home to make a full disclosure. Tell them everything. Brian was out the back playing with his new baseball. He asked Tom if he wanted to have a catch. Tom agreed. After a while Tom begged off and left. It would have been the right thing to do, to reveal his true identity, and to tell them what was happening. He couldn't do it. He just couldn't, so he wandered off. And then there was Emma. You're not supposed to fall in love with your target, but he did; that is, Tom Osborne did. Emma trusted him, and he betrayed her. He told her, Tom Osborne did, that he was an apron salesman, and that was a lie. He told her, Tom Osborne did, that he was in the midst of a divorce, and that was a lie. He portrayed himself as a genial church going young man, Tom Osborne did, and that was a lie. He was an attentive and worshipful suitor, Tom Osborne was, and this was a shameless, baseless, unforgivable betrayal of a woman who trusted him totally.

Tom Osborne was not a person. Tom Osborne did not have a soul or a conscience. He didn't die. He just evaporated into thin air. Tom Jamison, a happily married family man, was left with the guilt, the pain, the remorse, caused by the man he created. Tom Jamison had to accept the pain and remorse because he had a soul and a conscience, and he was totally responsible for the actions of the man he created.

Chapter Fifteen

It was five days before the election. Both sides had gone through a grueling campaign in an attempt to win over voters. Tony Brentwood was comfortably ahead by a margin that should win the election. Alfred Mitchell doggedly tried to close the gap; but made little headway. This close to Election Day, candidates tend to be a little nervous. With Election Day a matter of hours, it isn't easy to deal with unexpected charges; accusations that are made at the last minute. At this time, the Republicans were hopeful that nothing unusual would happen to change their outlook for a successful campaign.

In the wee hours of the night, while most of America was fast asleep, TELL Publishing started distribution of its special issue. Movement was by trucks and planes to make sure that widespread distribution would be achieved and America would have opportunity to buy the issue at newsstands and super markets. The issue was amply illustrated, showing Tony Brentwood in women's dresses. Tony was a cross dresser. There was also a large photo of Thomas R. Jamison, the investigative reporter who broke the story. This was a gratuitous slap at Tom, since he was on the fringes of the story and not privy to the real inside information. In a way, he was a decoy, set up by his own employer. Any adverse actions would be directed at him.

People were stunned by this revelation. It was so unexpected, and completely changed the dynamics of the election. There were those who would vote for Tony Brentwood, no matter what. There were others who could not see putting a man in the white house who dressed as a woman.

Pollsters were frantically trying to get a handle on what was happening. It was obvious that this had hurt the front runner to the extent that it was impossible to know, if indeed, this would cost him the election.

The Republicans were stunned by the news, but recovered to the extent that they went on the offensive, attacking Tell Publications for invading the privacy of a man's private home to take photographs. How they obtained the photographs was a closely guarded secret. Tell Publications replied, facetiously, that some unknown, public-spirited citizen left them on their doorstep. Senator Crouse promised a full-scale congressional investigation where TELL Publications officials would be required to testify under oath.

"These people are going to learn, the hard way, that you can't go into a man's home and take pictures," said the Senator

The next day, Saturday, the mood changed somewhat. Customers at the checkout counter, in food markets, were criticizing the clerks for having that trashy TELL magazine on display. In some instances irate customers took the magazines and threw them on the floor. The food market officials got the message. TELL was ordered removed from the display rack. At news stands, copies of TELL were out of sight. If someone asked for it, it was produced. Bundles of TELL were being returned to the publisher. People of either party resented the invasion of privacy. If a man, in the privacy of his own home, wanted to dress like Napoleon Bonaparte, this was his constitutional right. The Republicans kept hammering away, and they were starting to see results. It still was an uphill battle.

Back at the Brentwood home the feeling was hurt and betrayal. They had accepted Tom into the family, believed his explanation of being an apron salesman; a man who was in the midst of divorce proceedings, and involving Emma in a courtship that had no foundation. What he did was reprehensible, disgusting, and unforgivable. Emma, in particular, found it hard to believe that it could be the same Tom. The Tom she knew was kind, considerate, and loving. The Tom she knew would rather die than cause her pain and the deep disappointment that she was now experiencing. She was sure of that, and felt that there was more to the story than what they knew.

On Sunday pollsters were detecting a recovery trend in the Brentwood campaign. The election was still difficult to predict. In a situation like this, there are no reliable numbers that would be meaningful. The Democrats were very careful not to seem to take advantage of the situation. Although they were the beneficiaries of this revelation, it was a situation where it would be best not to refer to it in any way.

On Monday, the day before election, the feelings of voters were so diverse; it would be impossible to make any predictions. The pollsters thought that, through exit polling on Election Day, they would be able to spot a trend.

TELL Publications was having its problems. Bundles of the magazine were being returned in large quantities. The rush for the magazine never materialized. In addition, future issues of TELL would no longer be welcome in super markets and news-stands. Tom had said there would be a backlash, and there was.

Chapter Sixteen

Election Day, and the polls opened their doors, ready to record the will of the people. The day was clear and the temperature was warm. The sun was shining all over the nation. No rain clouds anywhere, and that was unusual. All of this indicated a high turnout. Who would benefit from the favorable weather conditions was a mystery. There was a feeling that Tony Brentwood was recovering from the initial shock caused by TELL's disclosure. Then again, Alfred Mitchell was in contention for the first time in the campaign. Clearly, there was no way to predict how a voter, in the privacy of a pulled curtain, would vote.

During the morning hours, a smiling Alfred and Martha Mitchell appeared at their polling station to vote. They were photographed with Alfred holding up the "V" for victory sign. This, in response to a reporter's question as to whether he expected to win.

During the morning hours, Tony Brentwood, and his wife Sarah Brentwood, appeared at their polling booth to cast their ballots. They were photographed and Tony was asked if he expected to win. He said that it had been a long campaign, and he had made sure that the voters knew exactly what his position was on every issue of concern to them. "The campaign is over and the voting is taking place. The election is now in their hands, and that is as it should be. My opponent and I will accept the decision of the people, whichever way it goes.

The town of Pitco, Maine was the very first to post results of balloting. Of thirty-eight eligible voters, twenty-two were cast for Brentwood and sixteen for Mitchell.

Samantha "Sammy" Lindstrom, aged 103, of Pawtucket, Rhode Island, was wheeled into the booth. When she emerged. She was asked whom she voted for. She smiled and said, "That's for me to know and for you to find out." She was assisted into a waiting car.

Throughout the day there was some commentary on radio and television, but most of it pure speculation. Pollsters were trying to spot a trend through exit polling, but it was a mixed bag. All they could say was that it was a very tight race. Favoring Mitchell were comments that, although they liked Tony Brentwood's ideas they just were very uncomfortable about having a cross dresser in the White House. Other comments favored Tony Brentwood as the better-informed, more experienced candidate to perform the duties of a president. Then, of course, there was the basic support of loyalists; people who were committed to vote straight Democratic or Republican, no matter what. However, once the voter is in the booth, and the curtain pulled, it was impossible to know how the revelation would affect the voter in the privacy of the booth.

As the day wore on, the people streamed to the polls to cast their ballots. At closing time, eight o'clock there were still lines of people waiting to vote. Although the doors were closed officials said that any person in line would be able to cast a ballot. After closing scattered results started to trickle in. The race was as close as predicted. Because of the time difference polls were still open on the west coast. The closeness of the race encouraged voters to cast their ballots. Sometimes, when a race is one sided, some voters on the west coast don't bother to vote since the result is public knowledge. This would not be the case in this election. Every vote would be crucial to the outcome.

The reporting continued. Some states went to Mitchell, and some to Brentwood. The announcers gave the total of electoral votes each candidate won, and how much were needed for victory. It soon became obvious that the count would go on during the night. It was reported that Alfred Mitchell had gone to bed. Not so with Tony. He was at Republican Party headquarters, monitoring reports as they streamed in. The results seesawed back and forth. There did not seem to be a clear-cut victory for either candidate. Finally, by the slimmest of margin, one candidate emerged with enough electoral votes to win the presidency.

At 6:32 AM, Anthony Brentwood conceded the election. He sent a message to Alfred Mitchell, congratulating him on his victory and wishing him well. Alfred was still fast asleep.

It was obvious that the cross dressing issue had made the difference, Tony had recovered from the low point, when TELL first broke with the story. It was a matter of timing. At first people were in a state of shock and disbelief. Gradually reason prevailed. In the privacy of one's home, a person has the right to wear whatever clothing he wanted. Certainly what TELL did was to invade the privacy of Tony's home, and publish the photographs in a sleazy, sensational manner. After hitting rock bottom, sentiment started to turn around. The public had recovered from the shock and was seeing the problem in a more sympathetic way. If the election had been held two days later, Tony would have recovered to the extent where he would have won the election handily. Unfortunately for Tony, there wasn't time to counter the initial reaction to the expose.

Without a doubt, the most vilified and hated man in the United States was Tom Jamison. He alone had wormed his way into the Brentwood household, photographed Tony Brentwood, and cold bloodedly stabbed the Republican candidate in the back. He alone engineered one of the most despicable acts in the history of our country. He alone dictated the outcome of the presidential election, taking it out of the hands of the voters.

The government was very much concerned about Tom's safety. Death threats came from many sources. They were worried about the safety of his family. Tom was whisked away by the FBI to a hotel in remote South Carolina. He was being held as a material witness to a forthcoming Senatorial investigation. A cordon of police guarded Tom's family. Tell publications had correctly anticipated an angry public by making Tom the lightning rod for the raging outburst from an incensed electorate. Without the intervention of the government, it is questionable whether Tom could have survived.

Chapter Seventeen

So, while the next president was putting on his pants, and other stuff, Martha was dressing hurriedly. The next first lady, by nature, never liked being pressured to do anything that would disturb her accustomed slow, methodical routine. But Ted Reynolds frantic call had awakened them; first to break the exciting news, and second, to urge them to get to the ballroom as quickly as possible. The party faithful was celebrating, and they wanted an appearance by the man who would be leading the nation for the next four years.

President elect, Alfred A. Mitchell, his pants securely fastened, and his first lady, Martha, both flanked by secret service men, and party officials, made their way to the ballroom. As they entered a rousing reception greeted them. They made their way to the podium and were met by another burst of enthusiastic yelling, clapping of hands, and pounding feet. He was their man, and had led them to victory. All through the campaign, he was always behind in the polling. He doggedly did what was expected of him, but was never able to close the gap. He went to bed with low expectation of success. Jubilant informers of the good news interrupted his sleep. He would have to have a talk with the Chairman of the Democratic Party, Ted Reynolds. What does a president do? How does he do it? When does he do it?

For Martha, there was a basket full of questions. The family would have to move to Washington. They would be taking up residency in that huge mansion with all those servants. Gone would be the provincial way of life that she found so satisfying. Bridge games with her neighbors would be a thing of the past. It would be a new way of life; meeting people with sophistication and worldwide backgrounds. It would be expected of a first lady, the wife of the President of the United States of America. She would have to adjust to a new way of life.

When the Brentwood story first broke, the democrats were just as stunned as everyone else. Although they realized that they would benefit from this news, there was no joy in the Democratic camp. They realized that this expose had put them strongly in contention. The nature of the TELL edition, and the carefully orchestrated timing, were enough to cause, even seasoned politicians, regardless of party, a feeling of revulsion toward the publisher.

To celebrate the Mitchell victory, a ball had been hastily arranged. The party faithful attended in formal attire, and there was dinner, dancing, and speech making. They celebrated into the early hours.

Ted Reynolds suggested a vacation for Alfred and Martha. Alfred had worked very hard, during the campaign, and his hand hadn't fully recovered from all that hand shaking. Ted arranged for a vacation in a beautiful, up scale resort in South Carolina There Alfred could relax and recover from the grueling day after day demands of a political campaign. Alfred was grateful for the opportunity to just do nothing. Well, almost nothing. Martha had some shopping to do, and Alfred went along to give his opinion on "what do you think of it? How does it look in the back? Do you like the colors? It's expensive. I never paid this much for a pants suit." Alfred survived the shopping outings, felt rested, and the vacation came to an end. It was time to go to work.

In the days that followed, Alfred had frequent meetings. For the most part, Alfred was more of an observer. There were cabinet positions to be filled, and this was a very involved process. Ted Reynolds was very much in charge. With him were four party top ranked officials. Aside from ability, or expertise in any particular area, the appointments were made based on standing in the party, geographical location of the state, support achieved in the recent election, or if some individual with prominence in the party flat out wanted a particular appointment. Then there were a large number of staff jobs to be filled. These usually were accompanied by strong recommendations from the party faithful. It was a mammoth job getting all of this organized.

In the course of the discussions, it was decided that Sanford Morse Clayborn, a veteran diplomat, well known and well respected in all capitols of the world, would be named Secretary of State. He would be responsible for all matters of foreign policy. For domestic matters, Sam Anderson, a no nonsense administrator, with an excellent track record on government assignments, would deal with all other matters. This would relieve the president of being involved with day-to-day affairs of the country. Alfred was asked if this was agreeable to him. Alfred said it was. He thought back to that fateful discussion he had with Dave Lambert. Dave wanted him to take vacations, play golf, and, under no circumstances interfere with the running of the Grigsby business. This was different. They wanted him to take vacations, play golf, and relax. They saw to it that he was fully involved, and fully informed regarding decisions made in the conduct of affairs of government.

Sam Anderson met with Alfred every morning. The President elect was briefed on what would be, the events of the day; who he would be meeting with, and what he hoped to accomplish at the meetings. Sam, from previous appointments, had established a good, working relationship with members of congress. He didn't always agree, but he was always very respectful of congress, and it was reciprocated. Sam Anderson, very quickly, established himself as a very competent assistant to the incoming President. He had a wry sense of humor that was very well appreciated by the media.

The country also got the message. With all the hard work finished. With all the "who does what" taken care of in the new administration, inaugural day was fast approaching.

Chapter Eighteen

It's inaugural day. The weather is sort of mixed. The sun is shining, and the wind is moderate. It is winter and it's cold out there. True to tradition, the outgoing President and the incoming President are in a car, seated side by side, on their way to the Capitol. The conversation is mostly small talk. The outgoing president was in a jovial mood, obviously relieved by the prospect of handing over the reigns of government to his successor, this serious looking guy with his eyebrows puckered. His record in office had more than its share of rough spots. It was time to let the next guy sit in the hot seat and make the difficult decisions.

Outgoing—I think you'll like it, living in the White House.

Incoming—I hope so

Outgoing—You'll hear talk about bats flying around making all kinds off noises. Don't pay any attention to that talk. I never did see bats. I may have heard them. The White House is a noisy place, even during the night, so you don't know what you're hearing.

Incoming—Bats? I never heard anything about bats. You sure?

Outgoing—Like I said, I never did see bats. It's just that it's talked about a lot.

Incoming.—It's hard to believe; bats flying around in the White House. I hope Martha doesn't hear about it. She'd high tail it back to New York.

Outgoing—It's just talk. I don't know of anyone who saw bats. It's just like the talk about the ghost of Abraham Lincoln floating around at the stroke of midnight. Here again, it's just White House rumors.

Incoming—I would like to talk to Abraham Lincoln's ghost. Maybe he could give me some pointers on how to handle my new job.

Outgoing—Do you have a dog?

Incoming—No

Outgoing—Very important. You should get a dog, and give it a catchy name. It's good for your image. People relate to dogs, sometimes better than presidents. If you find you're navigating in rough waters, it always helps to have a dog running around the grounds.

Incoming—It's that important?

Outgoing—It's essential. First things first, get a dog. Every one of your predecessors had a dog. You have to be careful. Don't mistreat the dog. Lyndon Johnson picked up his beagle by the ears. People were outraged. A dog is man's best friend.

Incoming—Watch out for bats; the ghost of Abraham Lincoln, and get a dog. Above all, be nice to the dog. You've been very helpful.

Outgoing—Always happy to be of service to a fellow traveler.

The car arrived at its destination. The two men shook hands. Alfred was quickly escorted to the platform where he would take the oath of office. He was asked if he had a family bible. Presidents usually take the oath of office on a cherished family bible. The Mitchell family did have a bible; a Gideon that they picked up in some hotel, but it was nothing special. No problem, a bible would be provided. Present were family members, Martha and the children some favorite uncles, aunts and cousins. Then there were, as always, upper echelon party dignitaries, and of course, the Chief Justice of the Supreme Court who would administer the oath of office. There was enthusiastic representation from Grigsby Holdings In attendance were Elmer Grigsby, David Lambert, Bob Benton, Ralph Esposito, Jerry

Silverman, their wives and children. Also present were Gerald Bream, and his new bride, Cindy. They, very wisely, left their pussy cats at home.

The United States Marine Band played a stirring march that delighted the guests. Then, from the West front of the United States Capitol, the Honorable Mark S. Wilcox, United States Senator, gaveled a call to order and welcomed those present, and those watching on television. The Rev. Caleb C. Higgins delivered the Invocation. The proceedings continued with entertainment and the swearing in of the Vice President.

According to the Constitution, the outgoing President's term of office ends on January 20th, at noon, and the newly elected President is sworn in at that time. And so the newly elected President, Alfred A. Mitchell, with his hand on the bible, took the oath of office.

> "I do solemnly swear that I will faithfully execute the office of President of the United States, and will to the best of my ability, preserve, protect and defend the Constitution of the United States."

And so Alfred A. Mitchell was, in fact, the President of the United States. He was hugged and kissed by his family. Martha could not repress her tears; they just flowed, she was so proud. Then came the inaugural address. The text was put into his hand with the suggestion, "Just read it slowly, and you'll be OK." Alfred did just that.

To close out the program there was a singing of the National Anthem by, none other than Ruth "Babe" Richards, who took time out from a busy schedule to accept this request. And, as expected it was beautifully done.

And, to continue the festivities, there was the Inauguration Ball.

News Item

New York—In a career change, Alfred A. Mitchell has relinquished his position as President of Grigsby Holdings and has accepted employment with the federal government. In his new position, Mr. Mitchell will be provided with a rather large home, known as the White House, in Washington, D.C. This building is fully staffed with cooks, servants, office personnel, highly qualified technical and management people, and gardeners. Mitchell and his family will live in this house, enjoy meals prepared by gourmet cooks, and have all household chores performed by the staff. In addition, Mitchell will have a chauffer driven limousine, and a private airplane with experienced pilots, to take him wherever he needs or wants to go. Also, he will have access to a summer home, Camp David, for relaxation from his arduous duties as commander-in-chief.

In his new position, as President of the United States of America, Alfred A. Mitchell will have this job for a period of four years, and will have the option of an additional four years, subject to the approval of the citizens of this country. All in all, it was a package deal that Grigsby Holdings couldn't even begin to match.

Reluctantly, Grigsby accepted Alfred A. Mitchell's resignation, and named David Lambert as the president. Mr. Lambert was previously the interim president, pending the decision of Mr. Mitchell. Since Mitchell decided to accept the government offer, the removal of the word "interim' from David Lambert's title no longer had validity. The Grigsby board of directors voted unanimously to remove "interim" from the title designation.

Said David Lambert, "I am very happy to succeed Alfred in the presidency. As interim president, I was keeping the seat warm for him, so to speak. Since he elected to do his bit for the government, there is no longer a question of his returning to Grigsby." He further commented, "If Alfred would decide to visit a Wal-Mart, he would go there in a chauffer driven limousine. I don't know what Wal-Mart would have that Alfred already has at the White House."

Elmer Dexter Grigsby, 2nd, Grigsby chairman of the board, and former president, said that the company will miss having Alfred's steady hand at the throttle, but they are fortunate to have Dave Lambert to succeed him and carry on the good work that was done by his predecessor. Mr. Grigsby further stated that he was confident that Alfred Mitchell would acquit himself and do a commendable job for the government.

Chapter Nineteen

Sam Anderson met with the president in the oval office, every morning. In these meetings the president was briefed on every aspect of the schedule for the day. Sam made sure that the president was fully informed as to what the meetings would be about, who would be present, and what they hoped to accomplish. He also made sure that the president fully understood the importance of the meetings. This information was given in a respectful, courteous manner. Sam also met frequently with members of Congress and kept them fully informed on matters of interest to the executive branch. In his dealings with Congress, Sam had a good working relationship. In his contacts with the media, Sam very quickly earned their respect for reliability and newsworthy material. Sam had a good sense of humor, a characteristic appreciated by the press.

Alfred Mitchell, at first, had very little to say at the briefings. He was so in awe of Sam Anderson's depth of knowledge on issues and people, as they related to the mechanics involved in making so huge a government work efficiently. He also appreciated Sam's persistence in making sure he understood what Sam was doing and why he was doing it. In time the president began to understand the work involved in the running of government. As a result of these briefings, Alfred found that he not only was beginning to understand, but was developing an abiding concern for specific issues he thought would be beneficial and should be adopted.

The transformation from a man who had no particular interest in world politics, or the regional and national running of government; being subjected to a grueling race for the presidency, and exposure to briefings by Sam Anderson, the president had developed to the point where he could question, to better understand relevant issues discussed by Sam Anderson. The president also received pertinent reading material that Sam thought would be helpful. All in all, Alfred was being treated with respect, and with all of the consideration that would be accorded the holder of so high an office. It wasn't always strictly governmental affairs. Sometimes they engaged in small talk.

"You know, Sam, what I find strange about this business of being the president is that I no longer carry a wallet. I don't even carry keys."

"You don't need them," said Sam.

That's what is strange. I don't buy anything, so I don't need credit cards. I don't open and lock doors, so I don't need keys. I don't drive anymore, so I don't have to carry a driver's license. I don't own the cars I ride in, so I don't have to carry owners cards."

"Being the president has its advantages. When you change pants, you don't have to transfer these items. You just change pants," said Sam.

"You're right, but what bothers me is that suppose I develop a case of amnesia, and wander away. I would have no identification with me. I could be lost for days, maybe months."

"No, not even for minutes. You're too well known. I wouldn't advise amnesia. If you have to come down with anything, I think you should give mumps serious consideration."

"I don't know, Sam, I had mumps when I was twelve years old. I don't think they recur."

"I never had mumps. Don't come near me. You may still be contagious."

"Too late for that. We've been in contact with each other for a while, now. You should have thought about it when you accepted the assignment."

"Can't think of everything, Mr. President."

Alfred thought back to his experiences at Grigsby. This was so different. Here he was, in the highest office in the land, the leader in a country more powerful than any other country in the world. Yet he felt more comfortable being president of the United States of America, more than in any position he ever held at Grigsby. It wasn't only the tutelage of Sam Anderson. Other high-level people, and cabinet officers were also valuable contributors. Ted Reynolds had been so right. It was a team effort and he was the leader of the team. Alfred felt the importance of his position, and he developed a real interest in the workings of government with regard to domestic and foreign affairs. With the campaign behind him, he was settling in to the presidency.

And how was Martha adapting to her new life as the first lady? She had a secretary who pretty much took care of everything. Occasionally she found herself doing first ladyfish things like christening a battleship by smashing a bottle of champagne across its prow, or cutting a ribbon to dedicate a new building of some significance. For the most part, her big interest was getting her bridge people transported so they could enjoy their favorite pastime.

Alfred thought about the advice he had received to "get a dog." They really weren't dog people so that suggestion was quickly rejected. Alfred didn't know if he was the first president, in a long line of presidents to occupy the office without having a dog. So what. He had much more important matters of greater concern. Occasionally the girls brought friends home and that livened things up a bit. Otherwise the Mitchells were able to continue their quiet way of life in the far from quiet White House.

Dealing with staff was no problem. In their previous life, Martha had a cleaning woman who would come in twice a week to clean the house. In between, Martha would do light housekeeping, dust the furniture and make the beds. Martha also prepared the meals, and afterward cleaned up the kitchen. And then, of course, there were activities that involved neighborhood driving; food shopping, visits to department stores, and taking Alfred's suits to the cleaners.

Life at the white house was so different. After finishing a meal, they just got up and left. Martha had some input in the planning of meals, but this was largely left to the culinary staff. Martha's days of making beds were over. Cleaning was routine. Whatever had to be done was done by highly efficient staff people. If a bulb burned out, it was miraculously replaced. No household bills, such as gas, electric, water, insurance, taxes, or whatever, had to be paid. Putting out the trash was past history. It was almost like living in a hotel. It was a luxurious life that wasn't hard to get used to. Since Alfred was involved in the running of a vast enterprise, he very quickly adapted to his new way of life. Although competent people capably administered much of government affairs, Alfred could not relax. He tried very hard to understand who was doing what and why. Sam Anderson was very helpful in that regard.

About the bats, and the ghost of Abraham Lincoln; "bubba meintses!"

Press conference.

Anderson—Good afternoon, gentlemen. I have this announcement to make. The president has been very much concerned about the problem of global warming. He feels that it is absolutely essential that steps be taken, in every way possible, to do whatever is necessary to correct this environmental imbalance. The world can no longer afford to ignore the growing mass of evidence that this is indeed a problem that is urgently in need of our attention.

Because there is so much concern over this problem, the president has asked Tony Brentwood to join us in doing whatever is necessary to deal with global warming. Had Mr. Brentwood been elected president, this would have been his first priority. The administration feels that it can do no less than make it its first priority. We're in this together, Republicans and Democrats, and we all have to work together to develop a program, and get it operative as early as possible. The president is convinced that Tony Brentwood has the vision and dedication to make a proposal work. We are very happy to announce that Tony Brentwood has graciously accepted the president's offer to join us in the monumental task of establishing programs that will reduce our dependence on oil.

Question—To underwrite the program, as presented by Tony Brentwood, would cost billions of dollars. Wouldn't that be a serious strain on the budget?

Anderson—At this point we don't know anything about costs. We don't know anything about programs. This is a completely new area. You can't talk money until you have a specific program that is agreed upon, and which has to be funded. Right now, the president's concern is to have an organization to deal with this problem. Tony Brentwood will be in charge, and we are optimistic that progress will be expeditious and fruitful.

Question—Will the program be what Tony Brentwood outlined in his campaign speech?

Anderson—At this point we have no plan. All we know is that we know what the problems are. Our aim is to correct these problems. How to do it will be what Tony Brentwood and his associates decide would be the best, and most expeditious, approach to these problems.

Question—It sounds like the plan Tony Brentwood suggested in his campaign talk has been discarded.

Anderson—Nothing has been adopted. Nothing has been discarded. When the president talked with Tony, there was no discussion of solutions, only problems.

Question—I know it's a bit early to talk about a plan that has yet to be considered. It seems to me that whatever plan is proposed; I wonder what effect it would have on the economy. Is there any assurance that whatever program is offered won't have serious disruptions on our economy?

Anderson—There are no restrictions, no parameters. It's impossible to predict what the final program or programs will look like. I can tell you this; the dynamics of the market place is such that we are constantly seeing new industries emerging, and long established industries, with products that have become obsolete. A case in point is the personal computer. It doesn't use any vacuum tubes. If it had to use vacuum tubes, there would be no such instrument as the personal computer. It would be much too large, experience frequent failures, and have serious heat dissipation problems. You are also witnessing the disappearance of telephone booths. Today, we carry the telephone booth, a cell phone, in our pockets. Regardless of what develops with the global warming program, changes are a constant factor. As new products enter the marketplace, other products become obsolete. There's nothing earth shaking about this. This is the constant change of a dynamic society. The programs that are developed will be, I'm sure, designed to drastically reduce our dependence on oil. There will be changes, but we'll have to wait until we have programs. At that point, we should have a good idea as to how it affects the market place.

Question—Why would the president invite a cross dresser into his government?

A chorus of groans is heard in reaction to this question.

Anderson—The president doesn't give a damn about this idiotic nonsense. He wouldn't care if he dressed as little miss muffet, who sat on a tuffet, whatever the hell that is. Next question.

Question—I see a time factor here. By the time this proposal becomes usable, years from now, the environment could deteriorate to the point where remedial action, of any kind, would be useless. We have the hybrid car. Why not make the use of this mandatory throughout the world?

Anderson—Every thing is on the table. Whatever helps, the president will back 100 percent. This is one approach. We certainly are receptive to hearing other approaches to the problem, or a combination of approaches. Tony Brentwood understands very well, the urgent nature of this problem. We are confident that he will do whatever is necessary to develop a program that will deal effectively with the problem. We can't make anything mandatory throughout the world. We are dealing with sovereign nations. There are countries out there which are as concerned as we are, maybe more so.

Question—We have our military all over the world, protecting the oil wells. If we get to the point where we are not so dependent on oil, wouldn't that relieve us of the responsibility of protecting our oil supply?

Anderson—It certainly would, but we would have to take it on a case by case basis. We will always have some dependence on oil. Our industrial and chemical companies use oil in the manufacture of many products. Here again, it's just too early to deal with.

Question—If I may switch to another subject. The Secretary of State has been making the rounds of all the democratic countries. We hear that he is advocating the withdrawal from the United Nations and forming a new organization composed only of nations that hold elections that are completely free. How is he doing?

Anderson—As you know, this was suggested by Tony Brentwood during the presidential campaign. The president is in complete agreement, and Sanford has been sounding out the various countries. On a whole the response has been favorable. Sanford has assured these nations that much good could be accomplished. Dictators have complete control of their people, and are only interested in maintaining an iron-fisted grip on their people and enriching themselves. Dissidents are harshly dealt with. They are usually killed outright, or thrown in jail under the harshest of conditions. To have them in an umbrella organization, such as the UN, has made it very difficult to pass meaningful resolutions for the benefit of mankind. By establishing a United Democratic Nations organization, we can have a smoother, more efficient way of doing the world's business. We're making progress.

Question—It seems to me that if the democratic nations withdraw, the United Nations, as it now exists, would be in complete control of the undesirable elements that would remain. I could see that this could cause all kinds of mischief throughout the world. Wouldn't it be better to work through the United Nations, as it presently exists?

Anderson—There are two very large, very powerful nations, not democratically constituted, that would remain in the UN, plus other nations with other forms of government. We, the United Democratic Nations, would make every effort to coordinate activities with the present UN. We would hope that the two super powers remaining would influence other UN nations to continue programs beneficial to mankind. As of now we're still in the discussion stage. No definitive decisions have been made.

Question—What would happen if a member state in the proposed United Democratic Nations is overthrown, as the result of a coup, and becomes a dictatorship?

Anderson—Once again it is a "what if" question. Obviously that country would not qualify for membership. It would probably be a matter of events leading u to the coup, and the involvement of the new organization. What the UDN or UN would do is hard to say, At this point, a United Democratic Nations organization is is a proposal, not yet established.

Question—With all due respect to the person who is so ably conducting this briefing, we would like to attend a briefing conducted by the president. Is this going to happen?

Anderson—The person who is so ably (thank you) conducting this briefing does so as an assigned representative of the president. I think it would be appropriate to say that every president, from Washington to President Alfred A. Mitchell, brings his own concept as to how the office should be conducted. Our president was formerly a president in private industry. His style of management is to have capable people on his staff, and to delegate to these people assignments he considers appropriate. Having said this, will he decide to conduct a briefing? He is the president, and he may decide to do so. This is his decision to make. In the interim, I think you will have to suffer through briefings from the handsome guy standing here before you.

(Applause)

Question—This is not a question. This is more of a statement, or observation, whichever is appropriate. I think the president should be complimented for his willingness to adopt issues that were proposed by his opponent in the presidential campaign. He shows a willingness to adopt proposals on the basis of the benefit to the country. His decision to invite Tony Brentwood to join his administration is a good indication that his main interest is the welfare of the nation.

Andersin—Thank you. I heartily agree. That should do it. Thanks for coming, and enjoy your day.

New item

Arab Oil Producer

Makes Huge Gift

In a surprise move, an Arab oil producing country contributed one billion dollars toward research to find a solution to global warming. The anonymous contribution was made through the Kichel Bank in Germany. Officials of the bank have been authorized to distribute contributions to jump start countries that indicate an interest in finding a solution to this very serious environmental problem. A Kichel Bank spokesman would not identify the country, but said that this country, whose only product is oil, was very much concerned about the damage the use of oil was doing to the environment. Their hope is that research could devise a system that would permit the use of oil without its damaging effects. If a substitute system is developed that replaces oil, this country will make whatever adjustments it has to make. The primary concern of this country is to do what it can to restore an ecological balance.

Why would an oil producing country be concerned about global warming? Why would it make a contribution that would be used against its own self-interest? What would be the most likely country to have made this contribution? How will OPEC deal with this new situation, apparently a member nation acting against the best interests of the organization? The questions were endless.

There were many answers to these questions. The feeling was that the environmental problem was real, and it had to be remedied. What good would their vast oil reserves do if the world suffered a breakdown of catastrophic proportions? The people in that country live in this world, and its people would be affected as well as all other inhabitant. Speculation centered on Saudi Arabia or Kuwait as the donor, but it was sheer speculation. No one really knew. As a result of this announcement, it was expected that OPEC would call a special meeting. Generally, the consensus was that the contribution was understandable. Perhaps it would be too much to expect if OPEC saw the light and voted to contribute some of its oil money in the cause of environmental research.

Senate Judicial Committee, in session.

Witnesses:

Peter N. Carpenter, Publisher of TELL Publications,
Harold E. Prendergast, Attorney for Carpenter
Harvey S. Culpepper, Editor of TELL Publications
George H. Heller, Attorney for Culpepper
Thomas R. Jamison, Investigative Reporter

(Excerpts)

The witnesses have all been sworn in, and are now testifying. They are being questioned by Senator Lindley B. Ruscomb, Committee Chairman

Seated left to right are Thomas R Jamison, Harvey S, Culpepper, George H. Heller, Peter N. Carpenter, and Harold E Prendergast.

The publisher of TELL Publications is being questioned by Senator Ruscomb

Senator Ruscomb—You have testified that the photographs in question were left on your doorstep. And then you testified that the photographs arrived in the mail. Which is correct, doorstep or mail?

Carpenter—Actually, Senator, there's no difference. The envelope, with the photographs, were combined with other mail that was left on the door-step.

Senator Ruscomb—Are you saying that the mailman dumps the mail on your doorstep, that he doesn't open the door, enter, and deliver the mail directly to a person? Are you saying that he doesn't enter your premises? Are you saying that he just drops the mail on your doorstep and leaves?

Carpenter—No, he does come in and deliver the mail to a person.

Senator Ruscomb—I want to remind you, Mr. Carpenter, you are testifying under oath. You are here to give this committee sworn testimony as to what actually happened in securing the photographs published in your magazine. You have made two statements; one that the photographs were left on your doorstep, and also that the photographs were sent to you in the mail. Which of these statements, do you say, is correct?

Carpenter—They arrived in the mail.

Senator Ruscomb—So when you said that the photographs were left on your doorstep, you weren't testifying truthfully. Is that correct?

Carpenter—Yes.

Senator Ruscomb—Who sent the photographs?

Carpenter—I don't know, sir, whoever sent them didn't identify himself.

Senator Ruscomb—Did you save the wrapper, envelope, or whatever packaging used in the mailing of the photographs?

Carpenter—No, we just didn't think of it.

Senator Ruscomb—You weren't the least bit curious as to who sent them and why?

Carpenter—I should have been. I just wasn't thinking.

Senator Ruscomb—Are you familiar with the Peepers Detective Agency?

Carpenter—Yes, we use them occasionally.

Senator Ruscomb—Did you use them recently?

Carpenter—I don't recall. I would have to look up our records.

Senator Ruscomb—TELL Publications paid Peepers Detective Agency twelve thousand, seven hundred and thirty dollars and eighty three cents. This was paid two days after the election. What did they do for you to be paid this money. You can forget about the eighty-three cents. It probably was for a hamburger.

Carpenter—I would have to check my records.

Senator Ruscomb—You have testified that the photographs were left on your doorstep, and that wasn't the truth. You have testified that you received an anonymous package in the mail. And now we have the involvement of a detective agency. Is there any connection between the agency and the production of the photographs? I think your lawyer wants to have a word with you.

>Carpenter in animated conversation with his lawyer.

Carpenter—Yes Senator, the detective agency was involved in securing the photographs. They were not mailed to me, or left on a doorstep. The detective agency was hired by me to investigate the possibility of securing photographs, which, if true, would be of a sensational nature.

Senator Ruscomb—Now we're getting somewhere. How did you know that Anthony Brentwood was a cross-dresser?

Carpenter—We didn't know. All we had to go by was that female garments were being delivered to the Brentwood residence, and the sizes were exceptionally large. Anthony Brentwood is a tall, well built man, and there is nothing on the usual dress shop rack that would fit him. This was a tip that came to our office. It never occurred to us that the garments were for him. It was discussed as a "what if" idea. It was one of many projects that we work on. It had been on the list for a long time.

Senator Ruscomb—How did you, or the private detective manage to take the photographs.

Carpenter—Entrance was made by the detective and an electronics professional on the day the site was being prepared for the first broadcast. There was a lot of activity with the installation of broadcast equipment. It was very easy for our people to bring in the necessary equipment; locate the office where Mr. Brentwood did his work, make the necessary installation, and leave.

Senator Ruscomb—How did the equipment work?

Carpenter—It was remotely monitored. When he appeared on the monitor, wearing women's clothes, it was possible to activate the photographic system. At times there was a change of clothing, so we had a variety of photographs. When we had all that we wanted, we waited for an opportunity to remove the equipment. This opportunity came with the third, and last, talk to the people. The detective and his electronic expert dismantled the equipment and left. The whole process worked flawlessly.

Senator Ruscomb—In all of the entries made in the Brentwood home, did you have search warrants?

Carpenter—No. Never thought about it.

Senator Ruscomb—Did any member of the Brentwood family invite you in.

Carpenter—No, of course not.

Senator Ruscomb—You entered a private home, with no legal search warrant, without invitation, without knowledge by the people who live in this private home, to make use of information that is none of your business. Is that correct?

Carpenter—TELL Publications is one of a number of magazines, sold primarily in super markets, that deals with sensational material. Subject matter varies widely from who fathered glamour girls babies, who is cheating on whom, and this candidate is a cross dresser. We get the information every way we can. People at the check out counter in super markets thrive on what is sensational, and we give them what they want.

Senator Ruscomb—Even if it's depriving your targets of their first amendment rights?

Carpenter—I don't know that we were. This is a matter for legal experts to decide.

Senator Ruscomb—You invaded a private home without a search warrant. You were not invited in. You entered with malicious intent. You used photographs illicitly obtained to do irreparable harm to the resident of that home. This isn't a matter for lawyers to decide. This is a matter for you and your lawyer to talk over.

Senator Ruscomb (to the editor, Harvey S. Culpepper)—How much of this did you know?

Culpepper—I was in on the decision to go after the story. As an editor, I felt it had enormous possibilities. I thought it was worth going after.

Senator Ruscomb—Did you know how the photographs were obtained?

Culpepper—No, I don't get involved in that area. As the editor, I take the material that is given to me, in this case primarily the photographs, and I put together an issue. That's my job.

Senator Ruscomb (to the Investigative Reporter, Thomas R. Jamison) What did you know, and when did you know it?

Jamison—I saw, and became aware of the photographs about a week before the story broke.

Senator Ruscomb—According to the TELL issue, you were the one who was calling the shots from beginning to end.

Jamison—That story was not the truth. The first I knew of the photographs was when Harvey Culpepper showed them to me. I begged him not to use them. He wouldn't listen.

Senator Ruscomb—(to Culpepper) Is that true? Did he beg you not to use them?

Culpepper—Yes, he begged me, literally on bended knee, not to use them.

Senator Ruscomb—And you wouldn't listen?

Culpepper—Of course not. I'm an editor for a magazine that thrives on sensational, scandalous, salacious, gossipy, tattletale news. Anthony Brentwood, being a cross dresser would, under any definition, be categorized as sensational news. I'm the editor of a magazine that has a unique specialty. If I didn't use the photographs, I wouldn't be doing my job.

Senator Ruscomb—Your job is to destroy people, to pry into their private lives and expose them to ridicule, facts that are not your business, or anyone elses, for that matter.

Culpepper—Senator, may I respectfully remind you, sir, that I am the editor for TELL publications, not the Readers Digest.

Senator Ruscomb—That is obvious. I don't have to be reminded as to who you are, or what you are. How soon before the election did Jamison learn about the photographs?

Culpepper—About a week.

Senator Ruscomb—He had no knowledge, at any time, as to how the photographs were obtained?

Culpepper—No, he wasn't in the loop. It was obvious to us that he had fallen in love with the Brentwood family. In our business, for an investigative reporter to fall in love with those he is investigating, is a no-no. You just don't do that.

Senator Ruscomb—When your infamous publication appeared, Jamison was prominently characterized as the gifted investigative reporter who had cleverly master-minded the operation from start to finish. Was that true?

Culpepper—No, it wasn't.

Senator Ruscomb—You are the editor. If it wasn't true, why did you publish it as the truth?

Culpepper—Actually, it wasn't my idea. Peter suggested it.

Senator Ruscomb—Peter Carpenter, the publisher?

Culpepper—Yes, Peter Carpenter. He said that we should portray him as the mastermind so that he would be the magnet for whatever criticism surfaced. This would take the pressure off the magazine.

Carpenter—I never made any such recommendation.

Culpepper—I have it on tape, and there was a witness.

Senator Ruscomb—So Tom Jamison knew nothing about the photographs, and when he was shown the photographs he was shocked by what he saw. Is that correct?

Culpepper—He was, yes.

Senator Ruscomb—He was so shocked, he begged you not to use them. And is that correct?

Culpepper—Yes. He didn't want them used.

Senator Ruscomb—And, knowing all of this, you gave him wide coverage as the clever investigative reporter who was solely responsible for producing the photographs.

Culpepper—We did. Yes, we did.

Senator Ruscomb—And you published this without his knowledge, or forewarning?

Culpepper—He knew nothing about it. He had no advance warning.

Senator Ruscomb—It appears that Tom Jamison was the only one who had the decency to speak up and try to inject a little morality among those who outrageously profit at the expense of innocent people. I am pleased that the super markets and newsstands are banning TELL Publications. I think our committee is well informed by the testimony we heard today. We have to take a good look at this category of magazine publishing. I have no further questions.

Senator Baird—I have a comment, and perhaps a question for Mr. Jamison. Listening to the testimony it occurred to me that you were the only one with a sense of morality, a feeling of what is the right thing to do as contrasted with your associates who callously and unfeelingly take pleasure in being in a business that profits by causing misery to others. You seemed to have used bad judgment by associating yourself with this sleazy organization. I am puzzled. Why did you join in with them?

Jamison—It was incredibly bad judgment. In the past, I have been mainly involved in the scientific area, and also subjects relating to health. When this assignment was proposed to me, I was told that TELL publications wanted a "fresh face." My first reaction was to turn it down. I knew that it wasn't for me. But then I thought it would be a change, something radically different from what I had been doing in the past. So I agreed to take on the assignment. I had no idea of what I was getting into. It was so bizarre. I just didn't realize that you just couldn't make yourself a part of the life of others without causing misery and heartaches. It was a tragic mistake.

Senator Baird—Did you, at any time, talk to them about resigning.

Jamison—Yes, I talked to Harvey about it. He said I was too well established with the Brentwood family to make withdrawal possible. I suggested that a story be floated that a Thomas Osborne was killed in an automobile accident, and that his body had been cremated. I thought that would work. The fictitious Tom Osborne would be history. Harvey didn't think much of the idea. He gave me three baseball tickets and told me to relax and enjoy myself. That was the only time I talked to Harvey about withdrawing. He assured me that I should just sit tight until after the election, at which time I would have fulfilled the assignment and could do whatever I wanted. I had no way of knowing that it would take the turn that it did.

Senator Baird (to Culpepper)—Do you recall this conversation?

Culpepper—Yes, I do.

Senator Baird—Do you agree with it?

Culpepper—Yes, I do.

Senator Baird—No further questions.

Tom boarded the plane to return home. He felt drained. With all he had gone through, the Senatorial Hearings were just one more hurdle that he had to endure. Even though the hearings had been favorable to him, he had this feeling of betrayal of people whose friendship he valued. He knew that they had trusted him as a close friend of the family, and he had caused them so much pain, so much anguish, it was hard to bear. Leslie had cautioned him against accepting this assignment. Being the food shopper in the family, she was more attuned to the nature of the magazines at the checkout counter. He regretted not having listened to her.

Tom sat there, munching on some glorified peanuts and sipping a coke. Since he first was shown the photographs, followed by the explosive issue, his brain could only think of his part in the whole unfortunate business, and the deep hurt that he had caused the Brentwoods and Emma. How long will this go on? How long does it take for a brain to shift to other thoughts, for thoughts pleasant and gratifying? They say that time heals all wounds. How long will it take for a brain to grow weary of self-incriminating thoughts? Right now the wound was raw, fresh. He will have to live with it. Give it a chance to heal. It will be good to get back to Leslie and the kids.

It was good to get back to Leslie and the kids. It was good to be back home. Leslie had watched the proceedings on television. She felt that he had done very well, and that the publicity will be favorable for him. It certainly will set the record straight. She was very encouraged. He hoped so.

About a week later, he received a brief note from Tony Brentwood. He had a better perspective on what had actually happened. He said that he could understand Tom's unhappiness, and suggested that Tom put all of this behind him, and get on with his life, as he was doing. He added that they all missed him very much, and would always consider him a very close friend.

Tom appreciated the note, but to respond would be impossible. He felt the closeness to the Brentwoods, and particularly Emma. He had behaved badly, and felt shame and remorse for the troubles that he bought into their lives. How could he face them now? How could he face Emma? He could have alerted Tony Brentwood about the photographs. He should have. He didn't have the courage. It was cowardly to run, and hide, and let them suffer the full force of the surprise expose. The note was really addressed to the Tom they knew, Tom Osborne. Tom Osborne was dead. The grief and torment caused by Tom Osborne was still very much with the other Tom, Tom Jamison. He hoped to do exactly what Tony Brentwood had suggested, to "put it all behind him and get on with his life." This was an ugly episode that would stay with him as long as he lived. No, Tom Jamison could not be Tom Osborne and resume relationship with the Brentwoods and Emma. Tom Osborne was dead. Tom Osborne had to remain dead.

Tom Jamison had difficulty reconciling Tom Jamison with Tom Osborne. It seemed to him as a play, a drama. It seemed to him as though he was an actor, in a performance in which he had the role of Tom Osborne. In this play, in his role as Tom Osborne, he's involved with the Brentwood family and falls in love with their housekeeper, Emma. Whatever happens during the play, when the final curtain is dropped, the actors take their bows, and everyone goes home; the actors, the audience, the ushers, the box office people, and the support staff. He Tom Jamison, the actor, goes home to his family, Leslie and the kids. Tom Osborne is no more until the next performance. That's the way it's supposed to be. Somehow, in the darkness of the theater, after everyone has left, Tom Osborne escapes from the script. He very soon finds the Brentwood family and Emma. They accept him as a real person. They are not aware that he is not a real person. He doesn't have a soul and he doesn't have a heart. He's merely a character in a play. What he says and does is word for word, and action; as conceived and written by the playwright. Tom Jamison is just an actor. Why should he be responsible for what an escaped character does? Why should he endure this heart-breaking guilt?

It isn't a play, and Tom Osborne is Tom Jamison. If Tom Jamison and Tom Osborne are inseparable, how could Tom Osborne commit to a deep love for Emma? What about Leslie and the kids? What about the Brentwoods and Emma? Tom Osborne is dead. Whatever commitments Tom Osborne made, he's dead. There's nothing more to be said. Tom Osborne will remain dead. For Tom Jamison the pain, the confusion, the remorse just won't go away.

But it wasn't Tom Osborne who professed his love for Emma. It was Tom Jamison, not Tom Osborne. Tom Osborne didn't exist. Tom Jamison did. How could he love another woman, when he loved Leslie? How could he make a commitment to Emma when he was already happily married? In our society, a man can't have two wives. Did impersonating Tom Osborne make that much of a difference in his relationship with Emma? Tom Jamison couldn't understand how he could have gotten into this mess. He thought, briefly, of consulting a psychiatrist, but only briefly. This was a problem that went way beyond psychiatry.

Was it animal instincts that attracted him to Emma? Is man, by nature, polygamous? Tom thought of Jacob in the Bible story. He had two wives, sisters no less, and two concubines. He remembered reading, somewhere, that, in Islam, a man could have four wives. In the past, Mormans practiced polygamy. This could be an explanation of what happened. It was pure animal attraction. His love for Leslie was all that mattered. Their marriage was all that mattered. Reason would prevail over mindless animal behavior. This would, in no way, minimize the compassion he felt for Emma. He had behaved badly. She had trusted him, loved him, and was betrayed by him. She was too fine a person to have this happen to her. He was unfaithful to Leslie. He will never be free of guilt. He had behaved badly, and he didn't know why, or how it could have happened. That was the basis for the torment that was tearing him apart. He didn't know why, or how it could have happened.

Alfred A. Mitchell

Looks at Alfred A. Mitchell

It was late morning. Sam Anderson had arrived early at the White House, and had just concluded a briefing with the president. After Sam left, Alfred sat there, in the oval office. He thought about the briefing that he had just received. It was no longer an educational process where Sam, very carefully, explained the issues in a way to make sure he understood what was going on. In this morning's briefing, he and Sam discussed problems and the most advantageous way of dealing with them. It was no longer a teacher / student relationship, as it was in the beginning. He now felt well grounded in the affairs of government to the extent that he could question and discuss issues with Sam freely. He realized now that he had come a long way in understanding what he had to know to be the president of the most powerful country in the world. He had been so naïve. He had no interest in government, foreign affairs, or anything else. His only interest was sports. Did the home team win last night? Now, his perspective had really broadened. He had a good feeling about being involved in matters that affect the lives of so many people; hopefully for the better. He felt presidential. He was no longer in awe of living in the White House. He was even thinking about being its occupant for a period of eight years.

He thought about the years he spent at Grigsby. They were difficult years. He had to claw his way to advance himself, to get the better jobs. Nobody lifted a finger to help him. When he was the Executive Vice President he introduced programs that didn't amount to a hill of beans. Cutting the phone bill, eating at your desk, and, of course, the obese women fiasco that had done so much harm to the company and Elmer. Even with all the problems, he sensed that Elmer always thought of him as the caddy handing him a number five iron. Then Dave took over and made all the right moves.

He was now more comfortable being president than in any position he held at Grigsby. The big difference was that he had been taken seriously and his contacts, not only with Sam Anderson, but with many others in the administration, were always respectful and helpful. He couldn't conceive of anyone demanding that he not make any decisions, even to the placement of a water cooler. Even Martha was taking more of an interest in participating in meetings of various kinds. Her secretary, Maggie, was a stimulating influence who enjoyed being with people. His daughters were very much a part of the college community, and doing well. All in all, the presidency wasn't nearly the awesome position he thought it would be. It was a job, and he had tremendous support from the rest of the team. For the first time in his life, he felt comfortable being in the situation he was in.

The Grigsby Guys

And The Mitchell Riddle

It was a routine meeting, with an agenda geared to business matters of importance to the company. It didn't stay that way. They digressed and soon found themselves trying to understand how their recent employee, Alfred A. Mitchell, could undergo so radical a change. He left Grigsby, as an incompetent, bungling, humorless administrator. He was now seen as the President of the United States, conducting press conferences, answering a wide range of questions, often with humorous asides, and exhibiting a broad understanding of domestic and foreign affairs. How could this be? How could one person undergo so radical a change? Have we misjudged him? They wrestled with these questions, and many more.

Bob Benton—I watched him on television at a press conference. He was completely relaxed and seemed to be enjoying himself. I can't remember one occasion, here at Grigsby, when he was completely relaxed and was enjoying himself.

Ralph Esposito—I think I have it figured out. They probably found a guy who looks exactly like Alfred, and is knowledgeable about most everything. They use this guy to conduct meetings, make speeches or whatever. The real Alfred is probable holed up in the White House watching soap operas.

Dave Lambert—It seems that way. I'm just wondering if he really had latent ability, and we weren't able to recognize it. I don't know what we could have done. I never saw any indication of any ability, latent or otherwise.

Jerry Silverman—What we know is that President Alfred Mitchell is the same man who spent many years as an employee of Grigsby. How the Democrats were able to take a man, whose limitations are well known to us, and transform him into a self confident, knowledgeable leader of our country? This is a baffling puzzle.

Bob Benton—I don't know what we're talking about. We seem to be blaming ourselves for failing to recognize Alfred's great talents as an administrator. I didn't see anything that would indicate latent ability as an administrator. It just wasn't there.

Ralph Esposito—I agree. I didn't see anything more than what Bob just said.

Elmer Grigsby—I always thought of him as the nice kid who used to caddy for me. He was over his head as the executive vice president. I didn't want him in that office. He just wasn't qualified. I tried to discourage him, but he persisted. I finally let him have the office, but only until we were able to bring in a person who was fully qualified. I made sure that he understood that it was a temporary assignment.

Bob Benton—He didn't look at it that way. He was determined to prove that he could do whatever had to be done, and done well. The problem was that he saw his role as an administrator with the objective to introduce programs designed to reduce expenses. The telephone thing, especially this business with the obese women; they were real disasters.

Ralph Esposito—Yeh, that was a real disaster. I warned him about using that lightweight crowbar. I should have whacked him over the head with a two by four to get his attention.

Elmer Grigsby—I guess I could have been more forceful in getting him to cut out these programs. I should have talked to him, maybe orienting him in the right direction. I don't know how much good it would have done. He just didn't seem to understand what was expected of him in that office.

Bob Benton—I don't know. You gave the office to David, and he's done a fantastic job. Yet, he didn't have the qualifications you were looking for. All of his background was in sales.

David Lambert—Thank you Bob.

Elmer Grigsby—You have a point. All of Dave's background was in sales. Yet, there was no question in my mind that he was the right man for the office. I called off the search and moved him into the position. The rest is history. Dave did a fantastic job. We just can't seem to get a handle on this vast change in a person. I have been thinking about it. As a caddy, Alfred had asked him for a job. I took him into the company. I wondered if, instead of being a manufacturer, would it have made any difference if I were a congressman? Instead of spending his years manufacturing, he would have been immersed in politics, a field in which he seems well suited. I don't know.

David Lambert—Thank you, Elmer. It's a logical explanation. It could very well be.

Jerry Silverman—The big problem seems to be that there was nothing in the previous jobs that he held that would have prepared him for the vice presidency. He was manager of the parking lot, and then manager of maintenance.

Bob Benson—Yeh. Somebody would report a clogged toilet. Alfred would pick up a phone and call the plumber.

Jerry Silverman—We were all very critical of him, bordering on the contemptuous. I think I was the worst. Now I'm puzzled, as we all are, I guess. What is there about the man that would cause him to do so poorly at Grigsby, and so capably as the president?

Ralph Esposito—That's the question.

Dave Lambert—I can't understand how we could find him so inadequate in his activities here at Grigsby, and yet see him in complete control of the presidency. He's doing well, no doubt about it. I agree with Jerry.

Elmer Grigsby—I should never have appointed him. I have to admit, as the president, he's a completely different person. If he walked into this room, I have no idea as to how I would react, how we would react.

David Lambert—I talked with him just before he left for the convention. I told him that I didn't want him to make any decisions as the interim president. I didn't want him to do anything that I would have to deal with when I would become president. I had no idea what he would do, but I had so little respect for his ability to make a right decision, I just had to get him to understand that this is the way it had to be. He finally agreed. So now he's doing well in the highest office in the land. I think all of us are baffled. We knew his limitations. That's why we find it so hard to believe what we are seeing is actually what we're seeing.

Jerry Silverman—I think that what we know of Alfred, and our experiences in dealing with him, we can come to two conclusions. The first would be that he was incompetent. Judging by the comments I've been hearing, I think we're all pretty much in agreement on that. The second conclusion is that Alfred is an intelligent person. I'm basing that conclusion on the way he is coming across in his public appearances. He is comfortable with himself, answers questions with ease, and seems to be enjoying being president.

Bob Benton—I don't understand. How could he be incompetent in the business community, and be a successful, intelligent president?

Jerry Silverman—Let's assume that Alfred is an intelligent person. We can assume that he is intelligent by what we are seeing in his activities as president. It would be logical that he was an intelligent person during the years he was here at Grigsby. I think the reason he was a failure here, was because he felt he had to initiate his own programs. Unfortunately, for him, his concept of what they should be was seriously flawed'

Bob Benton—I think we all agree. So what's the difference?

Jerry Silverman—With the Democrats, he didn't have to initiate programs. These were conceived and adopted by the Democrats during the convention. Being relieved of initiating projects made a vast difference. He no longer had the pressure of having to create programs that would define the politics of his party. This was already established. During the campaign the competitive spirit was awakened in him. The Republicans were the bad guys and they had to be defeated.

When he won the election, the Democrats appointed Sam Anderson to brief Alfred on the various issues that he had to know as the president. The briefings took place daily, and always with the greatest respect. The two men worked well together. Alfred was completely relaxed. Sam Anderson always referred to Alfred as the president wants this done, or the president would like to see such and such included in the bill being considered by congress.

Dave Lambert—I think you may be right.

Ralph Esposito—Alfred was elected president, and he will own the presidency for the next four years. Maybe he'll have it for eight years. How he got to be president was a result of a weird situation that got him nominated in the first place, and certainly the revelation before the election got him into the White House. How he got to be president is not an issue. The office is his, and I think the Democratic Party deserves credit for, very wisely, molding him into a credible leader of our nation.

Bob Benton—I think you and Jerry may be right. The Democrats deserve a lot of credit for recognizing that their newly elected president was capable of absorbing information under conditions where he is respected and on an equal footing with his mentors. A completely relaxed Alfred would be mentally conditioned to absorb what he was being taught.

David Lambert—I don't know. I thought he was like a loose cannon. I admit that I found it hard to like the guy, or even respect him. Obviously the new Alfred is a vast improvement over the Alfred we knew. What set of circumstances triggered the change is hard to say. The more he is integrated, and does well in his new line of work, the more we will benefit. I wish him well, and may the new Alfred continue to enjoy a good press.

Bob Benton—One development that I find interesting. The Grigsby Corporation could be looked on as a good source for future presidents. I think Elmer Grigsby should be our next candidate for President of the United States. All in favor say "aye."

Chorus of "Ayes."

The "ayes" have it. Elmer, you're the next candidate for president from Grigsby.

Elmer Grigsby—Bob, you can be my campaign manager. There is one problem. I'm sure Alfred will be running in the next election. As a

Republican, I would be opposing him. I don't think you guys would want me to do that.

Ralph Esposito—That shouldn't be a problem. Whichever way it comes out, there would be a Grigsby in office for the next four years. With or without your permission, I think I'll leak this juicy tid-bit to the press.

Elmer Grigsby—If you, or anybody else gets any bright ideas about leaking this to the press, that person will receive fifty lashes with a wet noodle. I am not now, or ever will be, a candidate for president. If I am nominated, I will not accept. I will not campaign. If elected, I will not serve.

David Lambert—Spoken like real politician. You just threw your hat into the ring. Hey guys, we have the next president right here among us, Elmer D. Grigsby.

Elmer Grigsby—He just left. He could probably be found, horsing around with his antique cars.

By agreement, the meeting was adjourned.

Chapter Twenty

It was a bright, sunny day, in late spring, a perfect day for golf. A little cool, but a great day to be out-doors. The president thought so. With nothing of a presidential urgency to deal with, the president soon found himself on the first tee, prepared to tee off. The first hole was a par four, with a dog-leg to the left. The green was protected by a rough area and sand traps.

The president teed off. The ball was hit well, but unfortunately, he turned a little, and the ball made a bee-line for the rough area. When the president arrived at the spot where the ball had disappeared, the caddy was standing over the ball, on the fairway, about six feet from the rough. The president was perplexed. "I saw the ball land in the rough, among the trees."

"Yes, it did. Apparently it ricocheted off some trees and rolled onto the fairway."